SOME

ABOVE
IT ALL

A Novel

SOME ARE ABOVE IT ALL

Holli Fawcett Clayton

GREENLEAF
BOOK GROUP PRESS

Published by Greenleaf Book Group Press
Austin, Texas
www.gbgpress.com

Distributed by Greenleaf Book Group

For ordering information or special discounts for bulk purchases, please contact Greenleaf Book Group at PO Box 91869, Austin, TX 78709, 512.891.6100.

Design and composition by Greenleaf Book Group
Cover design by Greenleaf Book Group
Cover photo by Eberhard Grossgasteiger on Unsplash.com

Publisher's Cataloging-in-Publication data is available.

Print ISBN: 978-1-62634-913-1

eBook ISBN: 978-1-62634-914-8

Part of the Tree Neutral® program, which offsets the number of trees consumed in the production and printing of this book by taking proactive steps, such as planting trees in direct proportion to the number of trees used: www.treeneutral.com

Printed in the United States of America on acid-free paper

21 22 23 24 25 26   10 9 8 7 6 5 4 3 2 1

First Edition

the first man to
summit Mount Everest in 1953

PROLOGUE

Keep going. You're almost there.

My heart is telling me all the right things, but my logical mind disagrees. The two opposing sides are engaging in a heated argument.

Turn back now. You can't do this.

Yes, you can. You are Marren Halleck. You can do this.

I am layered in warm clothing, puffy like a marshmallow, my face safely shielded like my troubled past. And yet it feels like I am taking a cold shower. I want to turn it off, to jump out of the misery's way. I cannot feel my face or my feet or my hands. The wind is picking up.

There is no way you can do this.

I turn back, but a giant gloved hand stops me.

And then I hear his voice, muffled through his balaclava.

"Please don't give up on me now."

I think of Brody. I didn't give up then, and I can't give up now. I must persevere.

1

miles away from my ...
the bed, making a beeline for the shower. After
long time before I can take a proper shower. I scrub every nook and
cranny of my body, hoping that I can endure the filthiness that I'm
sure the next eight days will bring.

I remove my duffel bag from the corner and assess my gear one
last time, just before I call the bellman to collect it. As I pull my hair
back into a messy bun, I give myself a pep talk in the bathroom mirror. *You can do hard things. You already have. This will be nothing compared to
what you've been through.*

A knock at the door signals the bellman's arrival. He places my
bag on a creaky luggage cart and disappears. I throw on my backpack and look around the room one last time, making sure not to
leave anything in this Tanzanian hotel. It seems I've collected everything, so I head downstairs.

The elevator doors open to the lobby, which is peppered with
people. It is bustling and loud. My tour group is supposed to include

only six climbers, so I wonder where most of these other folks are going. The smell of coffee beckons and I head in its direction.

The coffee bar is crowded. When I finally make my way to the large silver-and-black coffee dispenser, I pull the lever toward me, filling a Styrofoam cup with dark liquid. I look around for creamer, but there is none. The sugar packets look strange, shaped like bamboo-colored miniature sticks, so I opt not to use them. I take a sip of straight black coffee, something that I am not used to, and I almost gag. It is thick like motor oil and bitter like unsweetened cocoa.

Yuck.

Still, the jolt of caffeine breathes fresh life into me. As I brave another sip, I hear a call from what sounds like the voice of a local Tanzanian.

"Out Yonder Tour Company," he says, his forceful voice pushing us to congregate in a corner area. "Meet here for orientation and gear check."

I make my way to the small group forming around him. We coalesce, and he begins his speech.

"*Habari za asubuhi!*" he says as a smile expands across his face. "That means 'good morning' in Swahili, for those of you new to our language here in Tanzania."

A slender blond woman stands next to me and smiles. Her expression suggests that she is happy to be here, ready to hear more. I smile back, hoping to convey similar feelings. We turn our attention back to our enthusiastic guide.

"I am Simon and I will be your guide. Welcome to Tanzania, my native country!" His accent is thick, exotic and distinct. "Before you begin your incredible eight-day journey to the summit of Mount Kilimanjaro, you will enjoy breakfast here at the hotel, followed by a thorough equipment check. So please, if you will, make your way into the hotel restaurant, where I have reserved a private room in the back for our group orientation."

The six of us flock to Simon like moths to a light, and he leads us to our destination, a small room with a large round table and buffet line. We grab our plates and line up, moving through quickly, each of us piling on eggs and bacon and sausage and toast and biscuits in awkward silence. Finally, the blond woman behind me—the same woman who smiled at me just a few minutes earlier—interrupts the silence and introduces herself as Leslie.

Leslie subsequently introduces the Black woman behind her as ~ ~hina. I nod and shake their hands. When the three of ~~ ~~ ~~join the other

~~ ~~

courage I can muster, I take a seat next ~~~ and introduce myself.

"Hi, Marren," he says in a sexy, rugged voice that matches his good looks. "I'm Chris."

"Hi, Chris. This is Leslie. And Seraphina," I say to him, gesturing to the women who are now seated next to me. His stunning hazel eyes command me, drawing me in. The thud of my heartbeat pounds inside my chest. I hope he can't hear it.

He looks at the women I have just met and introduced to him.

"Nice to meet you, Leslie and Seraphina," he says.

Suddenly, the female member of the younger couple chimes in.

"I'm Claire," she says, her mousy blond hair dangling over her bony shoulders as she rubs the knee of the man sitting next to her. "This is my husband, Casey. We're from California, and we're on our honeymoon—as if it isn't obvious."

Casey smiles and waves. His hair is the opposite of Claire's: dark, thick, and curly. They are a sweet little duo. Something like Brian

Austin Green and Tori Spelling in the original *Beverly Hills, 90210* television series.

"Hi, Claire and Casey," the rest of us say in unison. Handshakes and greetings ensue as we sit huddled around the round table, ready for Simon's discussion to begin. I study the faces around me, realizing that, although I've never met them before, these are my people. At least for the next eight days.

I miss my person.

2

who I thought for sure would be dumb as a rock. Jocks usually were. But when our teacher asked for a volunteer to solve a homework problem on the board, and Brody boldly went up before the class to diagram a perfect answer, I was immediately smitten. It helped that he sat right behind me, and I could always turn around to pretend that I needed his help in figuring out how different factors affected the rate of chemical reactions.

It took him six whole months to ask me out. He wasn't your typical, arrogant jock, the kind that goes through girlfriends like water. He was kind, smart, and respectful. The boy that said "yes ma'am" and "yes sir" to his elders. Parents everywhere loved him, and not just for his ability to throw strikes. There was something good in him that didn't live inside of other boys with his caliber of talent. I'm not sure what I did to deserve his affection, but one Tuesday morning, just after chemistry class had ended, he stopped me in the hall.

"Hey," he said. "You know something? You have the prettiest eyes I've ever seen."

I was caught off guard. People often told me that my sky-blue eyes were beautiful, especially coupled with my long, dark hair, but still I wasn't confident enough to believe that I could attract a boy like Brody Halleck.

"You wanna, um, study some chemistry with me sometime?" he asked.

My "pretty" eyes widened. I fought the huge smile that was forming across my face, but it eventually won.

"Sure," I said.

And that's how our relationship officially began—on a Thursday afternoon, after Brody's mother greeted me at the door with warm cookies and Brody and I studied the similarities and differences between ionic and covalent compounds. Thereafter, we quickly became Marren and Brody, the Clear Springs High School power couple.

3

First, a drive to the Londorossi Gate, ~

paperwork to properly register. After that, a stunning drive through farmland with breathtaking views of open plains, just before we reach the Lemosho trailhead. There, we will hike through easy, beautiful forest terrain before stopping to camp for the night at a place called "Mti Mkubwa," or Big Tree Camp.

Simon speaks on, summarizing the rest of the trip, and somewhere along the way I lose track. I'm overwhelmed. There are too many places to go, too many things to see, too much of my stomach tied up in knots as I listen to everything that this trip will demand of me. Losing Brody has demanded so much of me. I don't know if I have the kind of energy—physical or emotional—to do this.

I bite off a piece of biscuit as Simon finishes up, and my anxiety worsens. At this point, I feel like a nervous rider, next in line to board the scariest of roller coasters. There is still a way out, and yet there isn't. I look down at my sweaty palms, and I wonder if I can actually do this.

You've come this far. You can't stop now.

Breakfast ends, and we file out into the parking lot, where Simon leads us out to a vehicle, the likes of which I've never seen before. It is an intimidating behemoth, a grandiose creature that resembles a large military tank. I can't stop staring at it as we gather around Simon, who is preparing for our gear check and weigh-in. I pray that I am under the fifteen-kilogram (or about thirty-three-pound) weight limit, which is Out Yonder's limit for the weight of the duffel bag that you can bring on the trip. Thankfully, mine weighs in at 14.9 kilograms (32.8 pounds), which is just within acceptable limits.

After the equipment check and weigh-in, we all board the behemoth. It is noisy and has a damp smell that reminds me of rusty water pipes or a high school locker room. I long to sit next to Chris the cowboy, but Casey and Claire claim the space before I can, so I end up next to Leslie. I suppose I am safer here. There will be less awkward conversation, less tension between us, or so I think. From the way Leslie first smiled and introduced herself to me, I'm guessing she's easy to talk to.

The behemoth crawls across poorly maintained asphalt at what feels like a speed of around forty miles per hour, maybe fifty at times. The pothole-induced bumps are often grueling, and the giant vehicle spits out a perpetual cloud of foul black smoke. Nausea sets in from the strength of the fumes; I feel like I'm being tossed around in a washing machine full of thick, black exhaust. The six of us— Chris, Seraphina, Leslie, Casey, Claire, and I—suffer in silence, for genuine conversation is nearly impossible on such a turbulent, suffocating ride.

▲ ▲ ▲

Hours later, I'm thankful to arrive at the Lemosho trailhead. No more jarring jolts or coughing fits, no longer the need to brace myself for what's to come or worry about taking in my next smog-choked breath. As the team unloads our gear from the behemoth, my stomach fills with tiny bubbles that burst inside of me; I am suddenly a nervous kid anticipating gifts on Christmas morning. The question tugs at me like a needy child: *Will I actually get everything I asked for from this?* I envision the mountain as some sort of Santa-like creature in whom I've placed all of my childlike trust, hoping for ̄ ̄ ̄ ̄ results.

̄ ̄ ̄ my duffel and assess my equipment

̄ ̄ ̄ handy list

jackets, mid layer tops, ̄
and a puffer jacket. There's also handwear ̄
gloves and insulated mittens. And headwear—sunhat, balaclava, wool ski hat, sunglasses, and headlamp. Personal equipment, too—trekking poles, sleeping pads, duffel bag, daypack, sleeping bag, pee funnel, portable toilet, water bottles, insect repellent, waterproof contractor bags, camera, water purification tools, toiletry bag, sunscreen, lipscreen, running shoes, personal first aid kit, medications, cough drops, earplugs, and hand and toe warmers. Finally, food items—Clif bars and energy chews.

It's all here, so I place a scribbly checkmark beside each item. Once everyone's equipment is unloaded, Simon waves us toward him.

"*Siku yako inaendeleaje?*" he says in Swahili.

Our crew of six stands silently together. Clearly, no one understands what he has just said.

He speaks in English now. "What I mean to say is, 'How's your day going?'"

Laughter—a shared language—breaks out across our group.

"Great," we respond in near unison.

A rush of energy crashes through me like a huge wave. Wearing my daypack, I'm ready now. My day *is* great. It gets even better when I look over at Chris and see that he is staring at me. It's the same kind of look that Brody used to give me, one of curiosity, like he longed to know what I was thinking. It always made me feel special to think that someone cared about my thoughts. I close my eyes and think back to the days when Brody made me feel the most special of all.

4

of Arkansas together. The drama takes my breath away.

We marry shortly thereafter.

Our wedding day is spectacular. We get hitched on a tractor, in the middle of Brody's grandparents' farm, just outside of Clear Springs. Someone has painted "Brody and Marren forever" on the side of the barn where we take what will be my favorite wedding photo. I am smiling in his arms, my raven hair pulled elegantly back into a loose bun, the sunlight beaming down in the background. My eyes have never looked so blue, Brody tells me, just before the photographer captures the shot.

After we marry, Brody's dream to become a major league baseball player takes us to Little Rock, where he plays with the Arkansas Travelers, a minor league team affiliated with the Seattle Mariners.

Our days in Little Rock are like puzzle pieces, each coming together slowly and neatly, forming a beautiful picture of our life as husband and wife. Brody loves being an Arkansas Traveler.

From the day he first puts on his team uniform—a sexy combination of white, black, red, and gray—he is happier than ever. He starts at pitcher in only his third game as an official team member, and things just get better from there. One win turns into two, two becomes three, and three leads to an impressive ten. His success on the pitching mound commands newfound attention from local fans, and the attendance numbers shoot up. In his rookie season, Brody goes on to win twenty games, the last one a no-hitter.

I'll never forget the magnetic way that Brody dictates the field during the last game of his rookie season. The way he stands there—a popular king reigning over his kingdom—his green eyes burning with fierce determination, sweat beading around them as he aligns his fingers perfectly on the seams of the ball and prepares to deliver a flawless curveball. His windup is incomparable, the ball escaping his grip in perfect time. I watch the look on the batter's face as the ball heads over the plate and sinks like a rock in shallow water. And then, the best part: the beautiful sound of the ball meeting leather, landing precisely in the middle of the catcher's mitt as the batter—frozen like a statue—just stands there, watching it pass him by.

A final strike.

A twenty-win season.

A post-game kiss in the middle of the crowd.

Our lives are magic.

Brody goes on to receive a contract extension and the potential to move up to the majors even sooner than expected. But, not quite three years later, things change dramatically.

5

that is full of life and devoid of malice.

one full of promise but also damaging UV rays. Thank goodness I remembered a sunshield: my University of Arkansas hat, which I proudly dig out of my daypack.

"Go Hogs!" it says across its weathered crown.

The minute I place it on my head, I picture Brody pitching at a Razorback baseball game, me cheering for him in the stands. I suddenly feel his presence, his hand holding mine. *He* is cheering for *me* now.

We melt into the rainforest under Simon's direction. I learn that this will be his 225th trip up the mountain, and I am in awe. I can't fathom *one* trip up this mountain, much less 225 of them. His experience brings a feeling of comfort, security. We are safe with someone that has done this such a great many times.

As we forge ahead, I savor the natural beauty that surrounds us. Gorgeous florals—including a type of flower known as the *Impatiens kilimanjari*—are everywhere. Simon stops briefly to point out one that is just beginning to bloom, and there are several "wows" from the group. Its seahorse-like appearance is breathtaking, its colors vivid—each flower offers up a stunning shade of red with four small, yellow spots across the bottom petals, an inspiring combination. I stare in awe, while Chris takes pictures of one particularly unique flower with his fancy, big-lensed camera, and the honeymooners snap what seems to be hundreds of selfies. Seraphina and Leslie continue along behind Simon, and I can hear them having some sort of intellectual discussion about the term *Impatiens*, which is a genus, as opposed to *Impatiens kilimanjari*, which is a species. Seraphina reminds Leslie that there are over 1,000 species of *Impatiens* in the world, some of which reside in their garden back home.

Smart, scientific women.

We press on, and I hear a loud, rolling croak, a sound that resembles a vibrating belch. I look around, curious to know where it's coming from. Chris taps me on the shoulder and points to the tree above us, and I see the source. Through the dense vegetation and moss that covers almost every branch of tree around me, there is a small black-and-white monkey with a white-framed face. It is a colobus monkey, Simon tells us, and its long, white tail hangs down from the tree as it continues to speak to us. It is another great photo opportunity for all.

Chris lurks behind me with his camera as we continue through the lush greenery. Another sound is up ahead, a steady cackle in the distance, almost like a constant purr. This time, I look up to see a beautiful bird, feasting madly on a piece of fruit from a native tree. The bird is a brilliant shade of Turkish blue with a yellowish-green chest and belly that is flanked in purplish red. He wears a Napoleon-like crown of darker, blackish-blue feathers and sports yellow and blue tail feathers that, according to Simon, are thought to bring good luck.

As breathtaking as this bird's features are, the most notable of them is a large, toucan-like beak that is bright yellow with a red tip. I've seen exotic birds before, but never like this, in their natural habitat, living outside of captivity. Tears of joy fill my eyes—Tanzania is even more amazing than I imagined. I yearn for more.

6

THE DAMP PATH THROUGH the rainforest unfolds before me, and everywhere I turn, I encounter a plethora of beauty. Sprawling ferns, sycamore trees, and junipers wave to me in the light breeze around us. A swallowtail butterfly—its black and gold markings resembling something like a giant bumblebee with over-sized wings—lands daintily on the petals of an adjacent *Impatiens kilimanjari*. Another animal—this one a blue monkey—clucks from the trees above us. It's as if I'm living in an ever-changing postcard.

Though we are traveling in a group, I begin to feel very alone. Each of the two couples—Leslie and Seraphina, Claire and Casey—stick closely together, but Chris and I remain solo. I feel a mysterious connection between us, but his silence baffles me. I wonder why he is not doing more to strike up additional conversation between us.

You can do it, Marren. You can talk to him first. But I can't. I am oddly obsessed and terrified by his presence.

He's traded in his cowboy hat for a Tilley one, green and floppy in just the right places. I see his new hat in the distance, and I wonder what to say. Perhaps I can ask him about his obvious love of photography. Perhaps that will be the perfect way to break the hot summer ice between us.

I watch him stop to take pictures, the ends of his thick hair sprawling from underneath his Tilley hat, the skin of his hands glistening with sweat as he wrestles with his camera to get just the right shot. I find myself staring at him often, admiring his tanned, leath- ͏ crevices have formed around his eyes. His look is ͏ something about him that makes me want

A gro͏ and other equipm͏ when we arrive at Big Tree Camp, ͏ in the dining tent, where tea and popcorn awai͏ ͏ that he is going to freshen up in his own tent before joining us ͏ snacks. I think about doing the same, but I am tired and sore and starving, and my growling stomach is now a tiny bit distended, so I head straight for the food.

The popcorn melts easily on my tongue as I place one savory piece after another in my mouth. My hunger slowly turns to bliss, and my stomach relaxes. Everything seems better until I realize that I am alone, sitting on one of the fold-up camping chairs that the porters have placed inside the dining tent. Seraphina and Leslie are engaged in a heated conversation, and Casey and Claire are admiring the T-shirts that they've just changed into that say "Just Married." Do I interrupt these couples' conversations? Would that be awkward? Inappropriate? What's awkward is sitting here by myself, munching on salty carbs with no one to talk to. I am tempted to leave, to find my personal tent, to dive into my comfort zone, where I can break free from this fear of exclusion. But then Chris appears, having wiped himself clean from the dirt and grime of our rainforest adventure, and he takes a seat next to me.

"Hi," he says. "Mind if I sit here?"

A wavy strand of hair dangles delicately over his eyes, eliciting a memory of Brody. Chris is attractive in the most traditional way—strong and athletic, muscular and tall, in impeccable shape—just like Brody, except advanced in age by about fifteen years.

"So tell me—what's your name again?" he says. I can't help but stare at him. The lines around his hazel eyes are even deeper than I first thought, and something about this makes him even more appealing to me.

"Marren," I say.

"Marren," he repeats. "That's a great name. So unique. I like unique. Where are you from, Marren?"

"Arkansas," I say.

"Arkansas?" he asks. "Where's that?"

"Seriously?" I say, crinkling my nose.

"No," he jokes, letting out a little belly laugh. "Of course I know where Arkansas is. I'm from Texas."

Texas. No wonder he reminds me of a weathered cowboy. His tanned skin alone is enough to intrigue me. Who is he? Where has he been? And why is he here, of all places?

"Texas," I say. "What part?"

"A small town about an hour and a half east of Dallas," he says. "Sulphur Springs."

I narrow my gaze. I know exactly where Sulphur Springs is.

When I was a little girl, my parents used to take me to Six Flags Over Texas in Arlington, a suburb in the Dallas–Fort Worth metroplex. My eyes would light up when we reached Texarkana, crossing over from Arkansas to the Texas state line, making our way along

I-30 toward Dallas. My mother would pack sandwiches and drinks in a small blue-and-white Igloo and play old-school country music on FM radio, because our 1988 Ford Aerostar wasn't yet equipped with a CD player. I always hated it when the radio station would be playing a great song, something like classic Willie Nelson or Dolly Parton or George Jones, and the static would slowly stamp it out like the remnants of a cigarette.

... I couldn't always count on hearing my favorite old-
... to end, I could count on the
... gas and a

...

of something else. ...
more, than my childhood memories of this ...

"Sulphur Springs?" I say, excitedly. "Do you know Colleen Hoover? She's from Sulphur Springs too!"

He purses his lips and his eyes dart back and forth, like he is seriously pondering my question. "I don't know her personally," he says, "but I know she's a famous author. My sister-in-law adores her books."

This makes me smile. He knows that Colleen Hoover is an author?

"I adore her books! And I'm from a small-town, too," I say. "I like small-town people."

He smiles at my words, his teeth bold and white. We are small-town folk, and we share this common bond. One that not everyone can understand.

"So tell me . . . what's *your* name again?" I ask jokingly, trying to sound serious.

7

An injury—a torn rotator cuff tear—

which sends him into a tailspin. He has gone from throwing curve-
balls and fastballs and changeups to tossing pills down his throat,
twenty to thirty times a day, and sometimes more. Every single day
since the day of his injury, he has required hydrocodone. Our lives
have become a hidden hell.

He needs work, so we move away from Little Rock and back to
Clear Springs, where everyone, including his father—the president
of a local bank—is willing to give Brody Halleck a shot at post-
career-ending-injury success.

Brody refuses his father's offer. I'm not sure if this is because
he can't properly function in the workplace or because he is too
proud to let Daddy jump in and save him. Whatever the reason,
he's managed to secure a few different jobs, only because of who
he once was.

Brody's most recent position—a work-from-home sales job with
good benefits—only requires him to be sober for most, but not all,

of the day. If he can stay coherent enough to sweet-talk folks on the phone from eight in the morning to three in the afternoon, he is free to escape thereafter. His form of escape involves taking more pills and washing them down with vodka, a combination that has led me into a new world of fear and devastation.

As much as I hate to admit it, I am no longer proud to be Brody's wife. I am terrified. Angry. Ashamed.

The Brody of today looks and acts nothing like the Brody I met as a junior in high school. The poison in those pills—and inside of those bottles—has made him into someone else. I am totally dependent on a man who is self-destructing before my eyes. My safety net is slowly disappearing. I am free falling into the world with nothing to save me from hitting rock bottom and shattering into a million little pieces, right along with him.

8

"You seem to have just ~~~

"Oh, uh—I'm fine. Just a little tired. Didn't get much sleep last night. Was too excited about all of this."

Chris nods and smiles and we chat for a while in the dining tent, and then Simon appears, recapping the day's events. Afterward, he dismisses us to our own personal tents to rest and get ready for dinner. Chris offers to walk me to my tent, but I graciously decline. I'm perfectly able to get there alone. Just like I made it here—all the way to Africa—*alone*.

I exit the dining tent, and bright red nylon summons me from a few feet away. I smile, proud of its distinct appearance. I purposely picked this unique color so that it would stand out, so that I would never mistake my tent for someone else's. Though it was practically brand new, fresh off the Amazon truck a few weeks before this trip, I decided to call it "Old Red"—the name of my mother's first true love.

Old Red was a male golden retriever mix with whom my mother spent the majority of her childhood. Oh, the stories I heard about that dog. He was apparently the most protective dog on planet earth, and smart to boot. Maybe even part fox, as red as his fur was, my mother said.

Her favorite story about Old Red was the time that he saved her from a copperhead snake as she played in a field near her childhood home, just outside of Clear Springs. I remember the way my mother's eyes would widen each time she recalled that experience, the way her face grew pale with fear when she came to the part where Old Red chased the venomous reptile away, but not before he courageously endured the snake's deadly bite. It was terrifying, my mother said. She'd been scared of the snake for sure, but even more scared of losing Old Red. Thankfully, he survived, and spent ten more years protecting my mother.

With a name like Old Red, this tent has no choice but to protect me on this mountain. I crawl into it, feeling the love of both my mother and her beloved canine companion.

▲ ▲ ▲

The porters have set everything up nicely, including my portable toilet, something I'd read was the best investment one could make when climbing Mount Kilimanjaro. I find my duffel bag, then dig out a package of baby wipes to freshen up. I begin by wiping my face and neck, then my arms, and I am somewhat appalled by the thick layer of dirt that appears on the wipe when I am done. I have never been one to enjoy being covered in filth. But out here, filth is part of the experience, a sign that I am actively participating in the greatest kind of outdoor adventure.

I am an adventurer. Pride swells inside of me.

Several wipes later, I am finally clean. I locate my journal, ready to document my first day's feelings. I write about the way my heart danced when the porters rallied together in native song as we walked into camp. The way I reveled in the sea of greenery around us as we floated through the rainforest like loose leaves in a sluggish river. The fact that, only hours into this expedition, I witnessed some of the brightest, most unusual colors I've ever seen in my entire life.

My thoughts move faster than my pen, and I struggle to legibly ̲ ̲ ̲ There are so many things I want to remember, includ-

̲ ̲ I first met Chris, the

"The Snows of Kilimanjaro, ̲ ̲ ̲ logue drawing me in. I make it through the first page when I hear Simon's deep voice call out, "Out Yonder Tours, meet in the dining tent for dinner."

I toss the book aside and emerge from my tent, anxious to experience our first dinner on this journey. I hurry along, hoping to find a seat next to Chris this time.

9

THE DINING TENT SMELLS FABULOUS. I vaguely recognize the smell, but I can't be sure. The porter lifts the top from a round metal container, and the powerful aroma tells me exactly what it is: beef stroganoff. This incites happiness within me, for beef stroganoff was one of my late mother's specialties.

My mother loved to cook, and she introduced me to the dish at an early age. I think back, remembering how she once said the words "I'm making beef stroganoff tonight" as she dropped me off at school, and how the anticipation of my first delectable bite of the beef specialty had coaxed me through another monotonous school day.

As one of the porters dumps a huge serving of beef stroganoff on my plate, Chris appears behind me. He smells fantastic, too, and I wonder if he stashed some sort of secret cologne in his backpack. I can't help but stare at his multicolored eyes. The layers of green, brown, and blue captivate me, the same way that Brody and his triple-threat combo of intelligence, athleticism, and humility once had.

The seven of us—Simon and our six group members—sit down at a table inside of the dining tent and begin to eat. Chris takes the seat next to mine. We converse lightly during dinner, mostly about the birds and monkeys and flowers that we saw along the trail today. Before I know it, plates disappear from the table, and after-dinner coffee and tea arrive. Simon instructs us to go around the table and officially introduce ourselves. He has purposely waited to allow us to do so, he explains, because he wanted us to have *individually* experienced our first full day of the trek—our first opportunity to bond with the land and the journey—before we began to officially bond with our fellow trekkers.

"Let's start with you, Marren," Simon says, pointing to me. I embarrassed even. I've never

cutting off my ability to speak. I feel tears brimming in the back of my eyes. Shame is bubbling up, and I'm terrified that it will soon expose me. I cannot tell them about Brody. Not yet. Not now.

Get yourself together, Marren.

"I've come here to prove something. I've come here to prove that I can do hard things. That I can survive. I can climb a mountain. All by myself."

The table breaks out in applause. I am surprised. I can't help but smile.

Chris goes next.

As he speaks, I cannot pay attention to anything but his eyes. And suddenly, a pang of guilt forms in my stomach. *It's too soon for this, Marren. You are not allowed to feel this way.* Still, I can't help myself.

"I'm Chris Courtland," he says. "I'm from Texas. I've climbed mountains 'round the world, and I'm ready to climb this one now, too. I guess I'm what you might call an adventure addict."

Laughter resounds.

"And I'm also known for my uncanny ability to tell a joke," he says. "Like this one. 'What do you call a funny place on a mountain?'"

We all stare, waiting for the punchline.

"Hill-sterical."

As corny as it is, another round of laughter follows. Something about the way Chris talks—his sexy Texas drawl, combined with his awkward sense of humor—makes me want to spend more time with him. I want to hear more, but he doesn't say anything else, so Simon moves on to Leslie, who takes her wife's hand just before she begins to speak. Her blond hair and pale, freckled skin contrast beautifully with Seraphina's dark features.

"I'm Leslie, and this is Seraphina. We come from New Orleans, Louisiana, where I'm a radiologist and Seraphina is a surgeon. We've been married for three years now. We made a promise to summit Kilimanjaro way back on our wedding day. It's taken three whole years, but we're here to honor that promise."

She smiles and turns to look at Seraphina, whose flawless skin glows, even in the dim light of our dining tent.

"And believe me, we *will* honor it," Seraphina says, smiling back at Leslie.

Both women appear to be ultra-healthy, in excellent shape, smart, and completely smitten with each other. I suddenly want to know more of their story, and I hope that it will unfold along with our journey.

Murmurs of "aww" and "how sweet" break out among us. Afterward, it's Claire and Casey's turn.

Casey goes first, pointing to his shirt.

"Well, as you can see, we're on our honeymoon." He looks at Claire as he says the words, and the adoration in her hunter-green eyes is apparent. She takes a hand and rubs her fingers through his thick, curly black hair lovingly, as if to show us how utterly in love she is with this man. "We were married last weekend. And we wanted to start off strong."

Smiles erupt throughout our group.

"We met in high school," Claire says, tucking a piece of hair behind her ear.

High school. My heart falls and my stomach flips. All of a sudden, Brody is sitting beside me, wearing his baseball uniform. I feel his presence, I hear him telling me that he loves me. I see a familiar love between Casey and Claire, the long-term "I'll never love any-

^ · love" kind of connection that Brody

Casey's mom ....

the look on her face is tense. Pursed lips. Worried eyes. Furrowed brows. Hopefully, her personality is not so uptight. *If it is, she's going to need to loosen up a bit.*

The conversation flows back to Simon.

"Well, I am happy to have you all here. As I said, I am Simon, and I am a native Tanzanian. I'm married, and we have a two-year-old little girl. Her name is Hediye, which means 'gift.'" He takes out his phone and pulls up a picture, then shows it to us. "Ooooohs" and "aaaahhs" permeate the tent. His daughter's face beams back at us with big, round eyes and exquisitely braided hair. I can see why Simon appears to be so incredibly proud of her.

We continue to dote on Simon's perfect little girl as he continues. "I graduated from a local university here with a degree in wildlife, and I am passionate about nature. It is my ultimate goal to ensure that your experience on Kilimanjaro is one that you will never forget."

I am intrigued by all that he is telling us, because at first sight, I would have thought that he was no older than eighteen. His baby face does a superior job of hiding the fact that he has summited this mountain 225 times—with a family and a wildlife degree, no less!

After the introductions, Chris's eyes meet mine for a brief moment. I quickly look away, not sure exactly what to say. He stands up as if to leave, then he turns back to me.

"Goodnight, Marren from Arkansas," he says, just before he walks toward his tent.

"Goodnight," I say back.

There is part of me that wants him to stay, one that urges me to invite him to join me in Old Red. But I know that's far too much for now, and so I shoo the thought from my mind. *We're not in college. Besides, what would Brody say?*

I trudge back to Old Red, and before I climb in, I look up at the night sky. It's a dark chalkboard speckled with tiny flecks of white chalk, a deep black abyss heavily populated with stars. I notice five particular points of brilliance, ones that I've been told to look for on this journey: the Southern Cross.

I've always been fascinated by outer space, and I've always wanted to see the Southern Cross firsthand. It's only visible to those in the southern hemisphere, and this is the first time I've ever seen it in person. From the books I've read, I remember that the stars in this constellation are between ten and twenty million years old. The closest one is eighty-eight light years away. With its rich history as a symbol of navigation, independence, resistance, and sheer beauty, this unique gathering of stars drums up something inside of me that I haven't felt in a long time—*inspiration.*

Energized by the incredible view of the Southern Cross, I climb into Old Red and pull out Hemingway's "The Snows of Kilimanjaro" again. I snuggle into my sleeping bag, flashlight in hand. Though it's hard to admit, I am finding that running from my past is more tiring than I thought it would be, and I'm exhausted from our first day on the mountain. Before long, I am drifting off to sleep. But, as I flinch in response to that momentarily terrifying sensation of rolling off a high ledge, my eyes shoot open. I realize it's not the feeling of falling that has woken me up this time, but instead the ghostly impact of knuckles against my face. No one is in the tent with me, yet someone is very much there.

10

BRODY HITS ME SO HARD that I cry out, and the sting spreads across the left side of my face like wildfire. For a moment, I am paralyzed in the darkness, but then I touch my upper lip and I taste the tip of my finger. It is salty like blood.

The light comes on.

"Oh, no . . . You're, uh . . . bleeeeding," he says. "What have I, uh . . . what have I done?" His speech is slurred, his voice muffled, but there is more to it than that, to why I cannot answer. And I cannot hear out of my left ear.

Something is wrong.

The pain on the left side of my head and face is worsening, and were it not for the bottle of wine that I almost finished earlier in the evening, it would likely be unbearable. I go into the bathroom and look in the mirror, terrified of what I might see but unable to look away.

My left eye is swollen shut, the white of my right eye is covered in bright red tributaries that flow into my pupil. The person staring back at me is nothing at all like the woman I'd hoped to become. She hardly looks human. Tears well in my eyes, and the red lines become brighter. If only crying helped.

He stumbles past the bathroom door and collapses onto the bed. My vision is blurred now. Is it the tears or the injury?

I need to go to the hospital.

I grab my purse and my keys from the top of my dresser and head for the emergency room, praying that I can sufficiently see and that I won't get pulled over for driving while intoxicated.

This will be the last time. The last time he ever does this to me.

This time, I will finally leave him.

stomach churns as I listen to the lyrics, and the knob to turn it off. I can't listen anymore.

I can't get away from this.

I am still a little drunk, so I take the back roads to try and avoid the police. Finally, I end up in the parking lot of St. Mary's Hospital, and I pull in between two white lines that feel like they are rescuing me. I am on safe ground.

I walk in and find the reception desk, which is decorated in red and green Christmas lights and a garland. There is a young woman sitting there with blinking lights reflecting off her face. Thankfully, I don't know her. I sincerely hope that she doesn't know me. She is staring hard at her iPhone, placing a green peanut M&M in her mouth as she studies the screen. She laughs at what she sees, then looks up to see me standing before her.

Her expression immediately sours. I am sure that my swollen, red eye is the reason for this.

I want to speak, but cannot. Thankfully, she speaks first.

"Hello, ma'am? May I help you?"

I nod, suddenly feeling the need to explain my appearance.

"I, uh, I need to see a doctor," I say.

"Yes, ma'am," she says. "May I ask what happened to your eye?"

"I got . . . hit."

She raises her eyebrows.

"All right, ma'am," she says, picking up a clipboard and handing it to me. "If you could just fill this out and have a seat, we'll have someone take a look at you shortly."

I accept the clipboard from her and select a seat among a sea of different emergency room dwellers: screaming infants being comforted by obviously frazzled parents, sneezers, coughers, and a host of others whose ailments have rendered them slumbering in chairs that seem cheap and extremely uncomfortable. I select a discreet spot in the back corner of the room, hoping that no one will recognize me, strangely grateful that my injury has rendered me temporarily unrecognizable.

My eye throbs as I fill out the paperwork. It requires insurance information. As a freelance writer, I have no insurance of my own—I must dig out my billfold and locate Brody's insurance card. This repulses me, because he is the reason that I am here.

I complete the form and return it to the receptionist, who is still staring down at her iPhone. She accepts it and assures me that I will be called back soon.

▲ ▲ ▲

Two hours later, they finally call my name.

"Marren Halleck?"

A petite, young nurse with long blond hair leads me into an exam room. It smells of alcohol and latex.

"So tell me, Mrs. Halleck, what happened to your eye?" She

stares at me with apparent concern, my chart in one hand, a pen in the other. Her turquoise eyes look familiar, and I'm sure I've seen her around town before. I'm hopeful that she hasn't seen me.

I return my attention to her question, which sends shockwaves through my soul. I don't want to relive the incident, but I know I have to. Tears are pushing their way to the front line of my emotions, and I can't hold back any longer. They spring from my eyes like mini-waterfalls across each of my cheeks.

As I grab the left side of my face, lightly finger feels

"All right, sweetie, sorry."

The nurse sets my chart down on the counter, then takes my blood pressure and my pulse. She jots numbers down on my chart and then turns to go.

"The doctor will be in to see you soon," she says, smiling. "You take care of yourself, now."

I can't believe what I'm seeing when he walks in. The familiar sea-green eyes and dark, thinning hair. A bit of a belly bulge, hidden by a stark white coat with navy lettering.

Samuel Caldwell, MD, it reads.

Dr. C.

One of my father's very best friends in the world. I was sure that he'd retired by now. Clear Springs is a small town, but still, I'd been hopeful that my ER doctor would be some young new kid who'd been sent out here, practically the middle of nowhere, as part of some state rural medicine program, the kind where medical students are trained for the purpose of serving in small towns like ours.

Someone who had no idea who I—or Brody—was. Unfortunately, all hope is gone now.

Dr. C's eyes meet mine, and an awkward tension fills the gap between us.

My father and Dr. C grew up together, right here in Clear Springs, Arkansas. At one time, they were best friends. Played ball together, went out on double dates together, shared many a lunch in the Clear Springs High School cafeteria together. These were just some of the stories my father told me over the years.

They would probably still be best friends today—despite the fact that Dr. C went off to school for several years to become a doctor—if it weren't for the accident.

"Marren, sweetie," Dr. C begins. "What on earth happened to you?"

I can't bear to look at him. He's known me since birth. He attended my wedding. He was a pallbearer at my father's funeral. How can I possibly explain this to him? I've worked too hard, for too many years, to convince everyone that my life—especially my marriage to Brody—is perfect.

Tears well in my eyes, but I keep my composure.

"I got hit by a softball," I say. My voice must not sound convincing, because he immediately furrows his brow.

"You did? This late at night?"

I nod.

His eyes seem to doubt me. My explanation isn't very plausible. Nevertheless, he goes along with my story. I suspect that he knows I'm lying, and he just doesn't want to make a bad situation worse by prying into the truth.

"Well, then," he says. "Let's take a look."

He removes his glasses from his head and pulls a penlight from his pocket. He shines it in my eyes and asks me to follow it.

"Hmmm," he says. "Your eye is concerning me a bit. Where exactly did the softball hit you?"

"Right here," I say, bringing a trembling hand to a sore spot just between the side of my eye and my ear.

"Are you having any other symptoms?"

I hesitate to tell him.

"I can't hear out of my left ear. It's muffled."

He takes out an otoscope and places it inside my ear. "Ah, I see why, my dear."

"What's wrong?" I say

ence some temporary hearing loss, but that should go away in time. Just make sure to keep your ear dry. No swimming, and make sure to protect your ear when you take a shower."

I nod.

"Any questions?" he says.

I shake my head.

He comes closer to me and grabs my hand. "Marren, you know you can talk to me, right? Rich would want that for you. I miss him every day. We all do." He gives my hand a little squeeze. "Just know I'm here for you if you need anything at all."

I nod again, thinking that I haven't heard anyone say my father's name in as long as I can remember. My father . . . once the dark-headed, blue-eyed chief executive officer of this same hospital. Dr. C knows me and my family well enough to truly care. Suddenly, I want to break down and spill everything. But I know I can't.

"Thank you, Dr. C," I say. "For everything." My voice trembles, but I somehow manage not to cry.

His warm smile reassures me as he leaves the room. But the second he closes the door, the tears come crashing down my face. The emotional dam that was holding them back—possibly even more fragile than an eardrum—has broken. I am living a life I never planned, stuck in a marriage disintegrating before my eyes.

11

longer than I would have liked, I m determined

for the challenge of a new dawn and the promise of things new and exciting. Breakfast is simmering somewhere in the distance, and my stomach is hungry, ready for food.

I pull out a change of clothes from my duffel and put them on, thriving in my fresh, new attire. Afterward, I head for nourishment, pleased to find the dining tent with hot porridge (something I've always called oatmeal) and coffee abounding.

I load up on porridge and find a seat next to Chris. His hazel eyes must look bluest in the mornings, I think, as the tender daylight first strikes them. He seems rested, happy, and interested in pursuing a conversation with me as I set my plate down next to his.

"I'm sorry, but that seat is taken," he says jokingly.

"Really? By whom?"

I can tell that he wants to continue the joke, but he also wants to talk to me and so he caves in.

"Just kidding," he says. "Please, sit down."

I gladly obey.

"So, Marren from Arkansas," he begins. "Why exactly are you here again?"

He asks this just as I'm shoving a spoonful of porridge into my mouth. He seems fascinated by this awkward, imperfectly timed bite I'm taking and keeps his eyes glued to my face. I swallow the porridge extra slowly while pondering my response. I can't possibly tell anyone here the truth, especially Chris. Not yet.

"I'm here to find something I lost," I say, marveling at my eloquence. This statement is definitely true, at least in part.

"And what's that?" he asks.

"What's what?" I say, trying to buy myself some time. I know exactly what he means, and yet I don't want to answer his question.

"What have you lost?" he says.

"*Habari za asubuhi!*" Simon's loud, deep voice saves me.

"Good morning!" Leslie and Seraphina respond in unison. The rest of us just smile and look around. *The smart women strike again.*

"Very good, my friends," Simon says, looking at Leslie and Seraphina. Simon still looks so young, so refreshed, nothing like someone who has spent so many daunting years braving the wilderness. "Are you ready for a new day of adventure?"

We all nod. Leslie and Seraphina, sitting across from Chris and me, join hands. *They've been ready for this since their wedding day.*

"A new day means learning something new, at least when you're here with me," Simon says. There is a clever pitch to his voice. "So, each morning, I will teach you a new Swahili word or saying. Today's word is *twende*, which means 'let's go.' Let me hear you all say it."

"Twende!" we repeat together.

"Fantastic," Simon says. "Soon, we'll begin making our way to Shira I Camp. We'll be leaving the forest behind and heading into the heath and moorland zones, areas of temperate grasslands with acidic soil, known for many unique kinds of low-lying and shrub-like vegetation. Be prepared for slight rain—the afternoon mist is sure to catch us. We'll end up at our next camp inside the large Shira Volcanic Plateau. *Twende!*"

"Well," I say to Chris. "Guess it's time for us to get going."

He looks at me, seemingly intrigued, the lines around his eyes framing a kind of curious gaze I can't seem to figure out. I'm sure he'd like an answer to his question.

I will never tell him what I've lost. I will only tell him what I think I can find.

12

DAY TWO OF OUR TREK does not disappoint. After breakfast, porters help to break down our tents and fill our water bottles. We gather as a group, each of us flocking to our match—Casey to Claire, Leslie to Seraphina, and, surprisingly, Chris to me. We follow behind Simon as we hit the trail again, and the warmth of the sun melts away my icy feelings of self-doubt. I find new confidence with Chris by my side.

"The tonic of life is human connection," I once read somewhere. At first, I didn't really understand what this meant. Now, I think I do. I imagine life as some sort of cocktail, like a vodka tonic, defined by its ingredients. The vodka is experience, and the tonic is connection. One without the other just doesn't seem to work. Experience alone, without someone to share it, is as harsh as a straight shot of vodka. The connection makes it tolerable.

For the last few years, I missed *real* connection in my life. Brody's addiction stole that from me. Each grueling day that I experienced in isolated hell—hiding from anyone and everyone and denying the truth—almost destroyed me. Chris has brought it back. He is the tonic of my Kilimanjaro adventure.

Chris and I make small talk as we enter the heath—an area that reminds me of the Texas Hill Country. I think of the time when my parents drove me from Arkansas to New Braunfels, Texas, for a weekend vacation at the Schlitterbahn Water Park.

On the way there, we drove through rolling foothills full of decumbent vegetation, much like what I'm seeing around me now. Funny that I am reminded of a trip to a theme park, because the area through which I'm walking now is something like the Disney World of plant life—a magical place full of distinctive flora and

explains. He pulls on one of the petals

seems unprepared for the challenge of confirming this scent. Her eyes widen in surprise as Simon nods to the petal, indicating that she should lean down and smell it. When she does, she takes in a long, deep breath, her eyes closed, and when she finally opens them, she gives a thumbs-up.

"Mmmmm . . . lemony fresh," she says. The group erupts in laughter.

Simon pulls off more petals, handing them out to each of us. I draw in a long, slow whiff of mine. Just as Claire has opined, I agree that the petal truly is lemony fresh. The smell takes me back to my childhood, when my mother would use a lemon-scented dryer sheet on the laundry. I smile at Chris as he smells his own petal, and he smiles back at me.

We journey on, eventually encountering torch lilies, or "red-hot pokers," as Simon calls them. Reddish-orange and fiery in color, they look something like the cattails back home, except they are spiky, not soft and fluffy. I immediately want to pluck them from their foundation and blow on them, like dandelions, but I refrain, knowing that their flowers are not so easily expended.

Perhaps most interesting, however, is the "old-man's beard," a gray-green lichen that looks like mossy, white hair. It grows on the bark and twigs of host trees, Simon explains, and can be used for medicinal purposes.

I snap a million pictures with my iPhone, and Chris continues to walk alongside me with his big, chunky camera. The incessant clicks begin to annoy me, but I tolerate them for his company.

Suddenly, we come to a small ridge and Simon stops us, pointing into the distance. My eyes widen at the majestic view. Thus far, Mount Kilimanjaro has not been visible. Here, you can finally see her, and our entire group stares in awe. She is beyond stunning, with her majestic, snow-sprinkled volcanic top and her broad shoulders covered in a halo of stratiform clouds swirling around her like freshly melted marshmallows in hot chocolate. It's love at first sight.

I feel Chris's hand brush against mine, and I wonder if the gesture was intentional. I look over to see him taking picture after picture, his mind clearly focused on the mountain, not me. Surely the hand brush was an accident. I remember the way Brody used to take my hand, to gently curl his fingers into mine as we'd walk down Dickson Street in Fayetteville, where he was something of a god. A baseball star. Any girl would have killed to date him, and yet he was mine. He was holding *my* hand in front of everyone.

I miss that feeling, of having someone feel so strongly about you that they are proud to hold your hand, for all the world to see. I look at Kilimanjaro again and feel a passion that I haven't felt in a very long time. I will summit this mountain.

I will proudly hold her hand, for all the world to see.

13

camp where we will sleep
edgy, bumpy, volcanic. Like braving blackish-gray, —
rain on the moon.

At almost three in the afternoon, we arrive at the campsite, where the porters have once again set up our tents in advance of our arrival. Simon dismisses us to our individual tents for rest before acclimatization exercises and dinner. I settle into Old Red and begin to journal again, my pen gliding swiftly against the pages. Like my life, the biomes here are ever changing. I wonder what tomorrow will bring, both here on this particular journey and otherwise.

Before long, I hear Simon calling my name.

"Marren?"

I put my journal away and emerge from my tent, realizing that it's likely my turn to acclimatize. Happiness envelops me when I look up to see Chris, who is apparently in my acclimatization group. Simon told us earlier that he'd be taking us up in groups of two.

"Hello, Marren," Simon says. I hear enthusiasm in his voice. "Are you ready?"

I nod. Chris nods back at me, a token of encouragement. His hazel eyes are greener now, and I marvel at the sight of their transformation. Bluer in the morning, greener at night, I have observed. But caught up in the optics of heath and moorland, I have failed to pay attention to their midday hue. I will have to study them more closely tomorrow.

Acclimatization—more simply put, giving our bodies proper time to get used to higher altitudes—is perhaps the most crucial part of our journey. Ascending too quickly can be deadly, even for the fittest of mountain climbers. This is one of the main reasons why I selected the eight-day excursion via the Lemosho route. It is a longer journey, but overall, a safer one. The more time we have to adjust to the altitude, the better our chances of success.

Tonight will mark our first "acclimatization exercise," or smaller-scale hike to a higher elevation followed by a descent back to camp.

"Hike high, camp low," Simon says as we scale up a weathered trail near our camp, and I suddenly feel short of breath. Surprise and disappointment swoop in to discourage me. The hours I've spent running bleachers at the Clear Springs High School stadium were clearly not enough, as I'm faltering to keep up with Simon and Chris.

"Come on, Marren," Chris taunts. "This is nothing. You can do it."

Simon lets out the tiniest laugh, although I can tell he is trying hard not to judge me.

We reach the highest point of our exercise and then begin our descent, for which I am grateful. Chris smiles at me, and I can't tell if it's because I'm entertaining him with my tremendous inferiority or whether he really likes me.

When we finally arrive back at camp, I feel better. Chris gives me a slight pat on the back and says that he'll see me soon, just before he fades into the vicinity of his tent. Simon asks me how I am feeling, and I assure him that I'm doing much better. I make my way back to Old Red and pull out my journal. I don't want to miss out on recording another small victory on this trip: learning to slowly acclimatize with Chris.

My copy of "The Snows of Kilimanjaro" stares at me as I write in my journal. I want to pick it up and continue reading, but my pen won't allow it. At the moment, there is too much to be commemorated.

As I finish the last words of my journal entry, I hear Simon call-ing for dinner. His Tanzanian voice is inspiring. Something about

very aggressive type. But Seraphina was transplant, and this woman is doing better than ever now. Modern medicine never ceases to amaze me."

The wind picks up. I enter to find Casey, Claire, Leslie, and Seraphina positioned together at the far end of the table. The two chairs closest to me remain empty. Chris is not here yet, so I take a seat next to Claire. As the conversation about Leslie and Seraphina's medical adventures continues, I can't help but notice the candle centerpieces: thin, fiery sticks placed in the middle of halved new potatoes. The tiny flames wax and wane, struggling to find shelter from the cruel new wind that now ravages the tent. Suddenly, Chris appears, and a handful of candles are immediately extinguished by the air rushing in with him.

Chris sits across from me, dressed in an olive-green fleece pull-over that accentuates his nightly green eyes. The conversation dulls, and Chris tells a rather unimpressive joke about my shortness of breath during our acclimatization exercise.

"What do you call a panting hiker on the way to summit Kilimanjaro?" he says, pausing for a brief moment. "Marren from Arkansas."

While he laughs, the rest of us stare at him in silence. Eventually, however, we all laugh, because Chris's failure is so awkward that only laughter can rescue him.

Dinner is finally served. One of the cooks hums a tune that makes me wonder what part of Tanzania it originates from. We feast on soup, chicken, and rice, readying ourselves for a cold night ahead and another physically taxing journey through volcanic wilderness tomorrow, including more acclimatization drills.

After dinner, I walk back to Old Red, and I feel Chris's eyes on me. Sure enough, I turn around to see him, his tanned skin still glowing in the fading light of day. I wonder why he is this close to me, why he is following me back to my tent.

"Marren, wait," he says. "Are you okay?"

I nod, still a little embarrassed by the way he exploited me at dinner.

"I'm fine," I say. "Other than the fact that I'm a panting hiker."

He laughs, but I don't.

I can tell that he knows he has hurt my feelings, and he immediately backs off.

"Listen, I'm sorry if that was out of line. Seriously. Forgive me?"

I give a half smile. How can I possibly say no to that face of his? I nod.

"Good. Because there's something I want to ask you."

"Okay," I say, waiting for him to speak. He hesitates and looks up, like he is contemplating something deep and powerful.

"I've heard it said that when we travel, we're either running to or running away from something. Which one is it for you?"

I picture Brody in my mind. The nape of his neck. The feel of his thick hair in my hands. The gentle weight of his lips on mine. And then, the smack of his palm against the side of my head.

I try not to cry, but the tears are too heavy as they congregate in my eyes. One falls down my cheek. Others follow.

"Oh, I didn't mean to upset you. Let's talk," he says. "My tent?"

It seems innocent enough, so I follow him inside. I notice Casey and Seraphina eyeing us as I do. I don't want any appearance of impropriety, but I want company, someone to listen. Maybe even understand.

He grabs one of his

14

I LEAVE THE EMERGENCY ROOM and get into my car, wanting to go anywhere but home. I weigh my options and realize that it's the only place I can go. I plug my iPhone in and select a song for the ride back. I choose Suzanne Vega's "Luka," a song from the eighties, just slightly before my time. It is about hidden abuse, the kind no one wants to talk about—all too fitting for my current situation.

When I finally get back to our house, I pull into the driveway and I sit inside of my running car for at least ten minutes, my weary head resting in my angry hands as memories of my life with Brody flash through my mind. Once high school best friends and lovers, we have devolved into disgruntled roommates.

I don't want to go inside, so I fumble with the radio. "Please Come Home for Christmas" by the Eagles is playing on my favorite Sirius XM station. I envision Don Henley singing this to me, because he has always been my favorite male singer. If only I could come home to Don Henley and not Brody—at least not like this. I picture Don singing to me as I walk in the front door. I want to smile, to enjoy this vision, to take it in as if it's actually happening, but I'm mentally and physically exhausted. The truth is standing between me and Don Henley. The truth is that I don't really have a home anymore.

I wish my parents were still here. I could come home to them.

There is a feeling you get when both of your parents have died. I cannot explain it, except to say that no one on planet earth loves you like the people who brought you up on it. When you lose the connection to people that actually give a damn about your existence, it's ͏ don't seem to exist at all.

ͳfully it's from my

been suckl͏

must still love this time of year because ͏

season. I study their admirable work: old oaks wrapped in tiny white lights, reindeer so real that you'd actually want to pet them, wreaths so classic in design that they seem straight out of *Southern Living*. I want to be inspired by their seasonal flair. To feel festive again. But most of all, I want to leave Brody. Because the spirit of Christmas has been replaced by the fear of my husband.

I walk into the house, my hearing still muffled, my eye still throbbing. The lights on the artificial tree are still glowing, the smell of cinnamon is still lingering in the kitchen, and a sea of our history together still sits atop of the living room shelves in the form of framed photographs. The story of us is everywhere. I walk over to the tree and survey the decorations. Several giant glass globes hang from its branches, many of them personalized, adorned with memories of our past together. My favorite is the hand-painted Razorback (in honor of our college alma mater). I also love the one with the Arkansas Travelers logo—a gift from Brody's parents in honor of his baseball career. But the one that catches my attention most is the ornament with the giant *H* in the middle, flanked by a *B* on the left and an *M* on the right. The *H* is for "Halleck," the *B* for "Brody," and the *M* for "Marren." It was a wedding present from one of Brody's mother's friends, one that was supposed to symbolize our special union—the one that we no longer have, thanks to the drugs.

I turn in the direction of our bedroom. I don't want to go in there. But I do, and I find Brody passed out on the bed in our room, which reeks of urine. I cannot stand to see him like this.

Tears creep in as I remember the day he won MVP of the state high school baseball championship, so many years ago now. He was so happy back then. So talented. So disciplined and determined. I thought of how handsome he looked in his uniform, of the crowd cheering in delight for our Clear Springs High baseball team. The way he found me immediately after the game and planted the sweetest kiss on my lips, throwing his arm around my shoulder, announcing to the world that a baseball championship meant nothing without the people you love to celebrate it with you.

That was my Brody.

Smart. Handsome. Kind. Respected.

I study the man that now lies sprawled out on our bed before me. Sunken cheeks. Bad skin. Incapable of responding to me, unable to get himself to a bathroom in time before soiling the sheets. This is not the Brody I married. Tainted liquid and tiny round cylinders full of personal hell have stolen him away. I feel my eye start to throb again, and I walk out of the bedroom into our guest room. As I climb in, I cringe with fear.

How is it possible to be married to someone and still feel this alone?

15

even sure I can climb?

It's all so surreal, how I even ended up here. At eighteen years old, I would never have dreamed of myself in this place. If you said Kilimanjaro, I would have told you that the only way I knew or cared about that word was from the 1980s Toto song "Africa." I have never had any interest in mountains. I am here for reasons I don't really understand. And now this handsome, cowboy-like stranger from Texas is offering to help me understand.

Part of me wants to tell him. Even so, I lie.

"Fine," I say. "If you really must know, I lost my parents in a car accident on the day after I turned eighteen." This is technically not a lie, but it is also not a truthful answer to his question.

When I say the words, he studies me sympathetically. I am thankful for the way his hazel eyes are looking at me, as if he is my personal therapist. Ready and willing to listen, to provide support and advice.

Suddenly, there is a voice outside the tent. I recognize it as Seraphina's—distinct and full of confidence. Exactly what I would expect to hear in a surgeon's voice.

"Chris?" she asks.

He looks at me with worried eyes. The same look that a child might give a parent if guilty of sneaking a snack from the kitchen without permission. I suddenly feel guilty, too, as though we've been caught like teenagers making out in one of our bedrooms.

Chris gets up and unzips the tent. Seraphina's commanding profile catches my eye. Perfect nose, proportional chin, plump lips, round eyes, square forehead. Her short, tightly coiled hair glistens in the new light of the moon.

"It this yours?" she asks, holding up a blue Nalgene water bottle with the initials "C.C." written on it in what looks to be black Sharpie.

Chris looks embarrassed, though I'm not sure why.

"Yes," he says. "Thanks. Guess I got distracted at dinner and forgot it."

Seraphina peers into the tent, where I am doing my best to hold still and disguise myself. I wonder if this is what a chameleon feels like when trying to blend in with its surroundings in an attempt to hide from predators.

Her eyes meet mine, and I realize that my effort is no good. My expression screams "different." I stick out like a proverbial sore thumb. I wait for Seraphina to say something rude, awkward, sarcastic, judgmental. Based on her pensive disposition thus far, I am sure she is judging me, the same way a perfectionist doctor might judge everyone around. To someone like her, I am surely subpar. In the tent of a practical stranger, contemplating the unthinkable on what is supposed to be a sacred journey to the summit of Mount Kilimanjaro. This kind of trip is supposed to be free of anything sordid, of any kind of one-night stands that might be crooned about in a bad country song.

"Marren?" she says.

I want to take cover in Chris's sleeping bag, but I know I can't. I want to drape his outer layer jacket over me so that I don't have to face Seraphina and her question, but that isn't a viable option. So I smile, as calmly as possible, and I respond.

"Hi, Seraphina," I say.

"Nice to see you," she says, to my complete surprise. "Next time, ̄ ̄ ̄ ̄ bottle at dinner." Her words are

the way Chris is looking

ger with him, but he understands why I cannot.

Seraphina makes her way back to the tent that she and Leslie share.

My conversation with Chris will have to wait.

16

ACCORDING TO MY IPHONE, which I've used sparingly along the way, it's five in the morning. Morning frost blankets my tent and the landscape around us. I put in my headphones and turn on a song, Carrie Underwood's "The Champion." Her powerful voice urges me to begin the day strong, determined, ready for anything ahead that might take me down—because I will get up and continue again, no matter what. I pull out "The Snows of Kilimanjaro" and start to read. The smell of freshly brewed coffee coaxes me from my sleeping bag, but I am too comfortable to acquiesce.

"*Jambo! And Habari za asubuhi!*" Simon's commanding voice says. "Time for breakfast. Meet in the dining tent as soon as you are able." I can't say no to the coffee smell any longer, nor can I ignore Simon's instructions, so I reluctantly unzip my sleeping bag and begin to dress for today's journey.

Frigid air shocks my body as I pile on fresh layers of clothing. The outside temperature is approximately thirty degrees Fahrenheit, according to my handy four-in-one thermometer, compass, barometer, and altimeter (one of my favorite purchases for this trip). I have

always hated cold weather. I prefer beaches and sunshine—hot rays
that beat down upon me and tan my skin as I sweat to the words of
a fantastic book. Today, I wonder again how I ever ended up here—
on a cold mountain, wandering into a world that I've never even
cared to know.

At long last, I make my way toward the coffee. I can't wait for it
to warm me up. I see Chris in the distance, seated inside the dining
tent, gripping a steaming mug and reading a book. He is hatless—
his hair slicked back atop his head, the thick, brown waves held in
_ _ _ _ of gel. When I walk over

Something tingles in my
unfinished conversation from last night, and I wonder when, if ever,
we will resume it. This feels like a TV show, temporarily interrupted
to bring you a special report, and yet we've never returned to regular programming. The two of us are alone in the tent now—perhaps
we will pick up where we left off.

I wait for him to say something, but he remains silent, his nose
stuck inside the book. I've never been a fan of silence, so I spew the
first words that come to mind.

"What are you reading?" I ask. Swirls of steam loom above the
hot liquid in my cup as I stir it carefully, then bring it to my lips.

He flips the book over and displays the cover. It's *Lonesome Dove*
by Larry McMurtry. I haven't read the book, but I've seen the TV
series a million times. Like so many people I know back in Clear
Springs—mostly guys—I am a huge *Lonesome Dove* fan.

Brody was the one to introduce me to this iconic book-
turned-miniseries. Something about brave men and the spirit of

adventure and the fact that some of the story was set in Arkansas seemed to appeal to outdoorsy Southern boys like Brody.

Apparently, these things appeal to Chris, too. *Not surprising.* Gus and Call, the story's main characters, were Texas Rangers—brave Texan men, just like Chris seems to be.

"I love *Lonesome Dove!*" I say, remembering how Brody and I used to stay up and binge-watch the episodes together, long before Netflix existed. "Best TV miniseries ever. Robert Duvall and Tommy Lee Jones were phenomenal."

"*McMurtry* is phenomenal," Chris says. "I've read the book many times. As good as the TV series is, I think the book is better."

Wow. I am impressed by his devotion to the written story. Most men I know would just watch the TV show and never even dream of reading the actual book. He flips it back over and begins to read again.

"So, Marren. I'm sorry we got interrupted . . . You wanna finish telling me what you were gonna tell me last night?" he asks, his eyes looking up from the pages.

His words catch me off guard. I haven't consumed enough coffee yet to process them. The answer to his question is too complex for an early morning breakfast conversation.

"Well?" he says.

I open my mouth to say something, but then Casey and Claire walk in, wearing some new ridiculous shirts that say "Kili Me Softly." I can't help but giggle. Chris drops his copy of *Lonesome Dove* and cackles loudly. Leslie and Seraphina file in thereafter, and we all share a laugh at the table as breakfast gets underway. The shirts successfully shift the conversation to a lighter place as we feast on toast, porridge, and eggs.

Those crazy newlyweds.

▲ ▲ ▲

I am finishing a second cup of coffee when Simon rallies our group again, preparing us for a hike to Moir Camp, our next destination. "Good morning!" Simon announces, his voice full of zeal. "Today, I'd like to teach you another new word in Swahili. *Asante*. It means 'thank you.' I want to thank you all for giving me the opportunity to climb this mountain once again, to show you all the joy that nature can bring. *Asante*."

We prepare for the hike to Moir Camp, which will take about six hours. I throw my daypack on, and Chris comes up beside me, his smile lurking in the shadow of his Tilley hat.

"Ready?" he says.

I'm ready.

17

WHEN I WAS EIGHT years old, I really wanted to go to the moon. I was obsessed with old footage, vintage pictures, memories of Neil Armstrong and his first walk across the iconic rocky, gray dirt. In spite of the 1986 Challenger disaster (something that happened just a few years before I was born), I was determined to ride in the space shuttle someday, to be propelled into a whole new world that existed beyond mine.

Back then, it was only a dream. Now, though I am nowhere near the moon, I feel like I am standing right on top of it.

Chris walks beside me as we trek on through the Shira Plateau. The silence between us is strangely uniting. I wonder what he is thinking, and I wonder if he is curious to know what I'm thinking too. The terrain is simple and relatively easy to hike. It is a flat, rocky combination of green, gray, and brown. We are strolling lightly, side by side, to the sound of rocks crunching beneath the soles of our boots. It is light and effortless, like walking along in a park—a nice reprieve before what I'm sure are more strenuous times ahead. It feels good. My life hasn't felt this uncomplicated for a very long time.

Simon stops us along the way to explain the history of the Shira Plateau. Mount Kilimanjaro is made up of three volcanic cones: Mawenzi, Kibo, and Shira. Kibo is the highest. It once erupted and collapsed into Shira, leaving a large crater. Over the years, Kibo erupted again and again, filling the crater with ash and lava that, over time, formed the plateau. Though Mawenzi and Shira are extinct, Kibo is currently dormant and could still erupt again someday. A slither of panic jolts me when I hear this.

We soldier on, and Chris falls behind me, his pace slowed by his ~~.. .. .. the vegetation is sparse but beautiful. There~~

on the right path.

Chris catches up with me, and we come to a uniquely shaped cairn, which resembles a jumbled Buddha statue. Chris asks me what I think it might be. When I say a rocky Buddha, he laughs a little. The person who created this rock formation has brought two strangers a tiny bit of joy.

About three hours in, we stop to have lunch at Shira 2 Camp. Simon pulls out something called an oximeter and measures our oxygen levels. "This is the point of the Lemosho Route where many begin to experience altitude sickness," he informs us. Simon then points to an access road in the distance. "This is the emergency evacuation route down the mountain. If anyone gets sick or injured, emergency vehicles can make their way up to this point to evacuate them. We are now at 12,500 feet."

As we begin to eat our soup, sandwiches, and cookies, I feel a bit short of breath. Thankfully, Chris is next to me, and the sight of his

Tilley hat is strangely reassuring. Seraphina sits on the other side of me, eating her sandwich as precisely as she listened to Simon's Swahili lesson this morning. I try my best to maintain composure as I struggle for breath. Fear rises up within me as I feel a sharp pain in my head and suddenly feel woozy. I reach out to catch myself on Seraphina, and she immediately goes into physician mode.

"Marren," she says in her commanding deep voice. "Are you okay?"

Blackness closes in around me. And then I fall to the ground.

18

puts his arms a—

He squeezes me tighter, drawing my back into his chest as he whispers into my ear. I wince at his smell, a putrid combination of alcohol and urine.

"I'm so sorry. I'm so sorry, Mare."

I am scared to move. I don't know if he is still high or drunk or some sort of combination thereof. He begins to sob, and I feel something wet fall onto my skin, piercing through the thinning strands of hair on the backside of my head.

His sobs increase in frequency and volume. I remain silent. What am I supposed to say?

Finally, I wriggle myself from his arms and turn to face him. My eye burns. I still can't hear much out of my left ear. When he sees my face, he gasps.

"Oh, my god. Did I—"

All I can do is nod. I still cannot speak. The words won't leave my mouth—I am terrified of the reaction they might bring.

"Oh, Mare," he says, still sobbing. "How could I hurt you like this? What have I done to my sweet girl?"

I can't answer his question for him, and the answer is far too complex for a single response.

His face is swollen from crying and his hair a greasy mess, and I suddenly begin to feel sorry for him. My Brody. I'm looking at my Brody. And yet at the same time, I'm staring at a desperate stranger, one who can no longer properly care for himself. Basic hygiene is gone. Though he seems sober now, I can't be sure. It is day-to-day, hour-to-hour, minute-to-minute. He's making sense, though, and I'm grateful for this.

Suddenly, words exit my mouth.

"I have to go," I say. "Doctor's appointment. They have to look at my ear. The ER doctor scheduled a follow-up this morning with a new otolaryngologist."

Terror flares up in Brody's eyes.

"ER doctor?" he asks.

"Yes, I drove myself to the emergency room last night. But don't worry," I say. "I told Dr. C that I got hit by a softball." The words come out before I realize that I've said them.

Brody crinkles his face when he hears "Dr. C." He is obviously guilty, ashamed. I know that look too well.

"You saw Dr. C?" he asks. "Did you tell him that I—"

"Don't worry," I assure him. "I told him that I got hit by a softball."

Brody is silent. He puts his head in his hands and begins to sob quietly.

"I'll never forgive myself for this," he says, speaking into his hands.

I may never forgive you for this either.

I grab a rubber band from the guest room nightstand and tie my hair back. "I'm going to shower," I say. "My appointment is at two." This reminds me that I will have to proceed with caution, for I cannot get my ear wet, at least not until my eardrum heals.

Brody looks up and catches my gaze as I get up out of the bed.

We don't speak. The silence says it all. Our marriage is on the brink of collapse.

I head for our master bathroom and I lock the door behind me, and I break down as I turn on the water to the hottest setting, hoping the steam will clear away this heartbreak.

▲ ▲ ▲

the new otolaryngologist in town—is not

Dad. Sister. Brother. Cousin. Aunt. Uncle. Even a son or a daughter, though I know that would be complicated in this particular situation.

I fiddle with XM radio again, and "Away from the Sun" by Three Doors Down comes on. I sing along to the lyrics. Something about belting out the words empowers me—finding myself away from the sun, in such a dark place that no one can see me and I can no longer feel anything. With each passing second, I feel like I'm falling farther into the same kind of darkness that the band is singing about, and no one can stop me. There's nowhere to turn. I have some friends here in Clear Springs, but I am too ashamed to call them. They will judge. I know this, because they are the kind of friends that only agree to go have dinner with you at the Country Club because you're married to a former baseball legend. If I weren't married to Brody, I wouldn't count.

For a moment, I think of calling Brody's parents, George and Trish. Of telling them everything, finally coming clean. They know that something is wrong, but until now, I've been skilled at hiding the true extent of it. To them, it's just a season of depression that will someday disappear, along with the pills. At least that's what Brody tells them—every single time. But I know the truth. I know where this is headed if something doesn't change soon. The problem is that I am the only one that knows this, and so I carry a burden that is tantamount to a prison sentence.

Solitary confinement, in fact.

No family I can tell. No friends I can talk to. Only "Away from the Sun," here with me on the radio. I sing louder.

I stop at a local bookstore—Mrs. Cane's Books and Such—and search for a book to help me escape my life. I find a latest bestseller, one about a husband and wife who decide to ditch their lives in the U.S. and sail around the world together. I open it and begin to read, and it immediately takes me to warm, sunny places in the western Caribbean that I'm sure I will never see. Not in this lifetime. Not in my current marriage.

I close the book and put it away. This fictional couple is happy, with hope and a future ahead. With hydrocodone at the helm, Brody and I can never accomplish something like this. No wonder they call it fiction.

I leave Books and Such and head to my car, checking my phone as I do. I look down to see a text from Brody, a rare occurrence. We have grown so far apart that even daily electronic communication has fallen by the wayside. The words on my phone screen intrigue and haunt me.

My sweet Mare, I am so sorry. I know what I have to do now. I hope you can forgive me for everything.

I start the car and head for the house. I find myself driving faster, my mind conjuring happier memories of days gone by. Junior prom and the strapless, hip-hugging, ruched black dress that gained a thousand compliments. Senior prom, one month to the day after the accident. Brody's strong arms as they led me away, words he whispered into my ear that would cure the suicidal thoughts. Brody's encouragement—each and every time I'd falter, longing to converse with parents I'd never see again.

Now, Brody is incapable of this kind of support. He might not ever be capable of it again. I miss my best friend, my cheerleader. Hopelessness seeps into me as I drive on through the streets of Clear Springs, avoiding home with every ounce of energy I've

resentment and reg...

me. Once again, I don't want to get out of the car. I don't want to go inside of that house. There is a feeling in my gut that is telling me something I don't want to know.

My hand shakes as I fish my keys from my purse. Forever comes and goes as I attempt to stick the key in the lock. Finally, I hear the click and turn the knob. There is a silence in the house that disturbs me.

I walk toward the bedroom, calling his name.

"Brody?" I say.

There is no answer.

"Brody?" I try again, louder this time.

He still doesn't respond. Normally, this would bring me comfort, because I wouldn't have to fear him. I can always simply assume he is asleep, dozing peacefully after his latest dose of pills. But something feels different now. I walk faster, expecting to find him snoring, passed out in our bed. Instead, I find him on our bedroom floor, and he is not breathing.

After all that he has done to me, I find myself desperate to save him, but I cannot. I rush to begin CPR, pressing on his chest to the beat of "Staying Alive." I try it, again and again. He doesn't speak. He doesn't respond at all.

He is slowly turning cold, and I know what is happening, though I don't want to accept it. I grab my phone and dial 911. *This is it. This is finally the end.*

A woman's voice sounds faint on the other end of the line. I can barely hear what she is saying, but I think it is something like "911, can I help you?"

Still desperately performing compressions, I reach one hand over to the phone and put it on speaker. "911, can I help you?" the woman asks again.

"Send an ambulance! Please! My husband is unconscious and I can't wake him up!" My voice is frantic. The woman responds calmly.

"What's your address, ma'am?"

"1517 Quiet Oaks Lane. Please! Help me! Brody, wake up!"

He is still unresponsive, but I refuse to give up. More compressions. *Please, Brody, you have to stay alive.*

19

my full water bottle, ͺͺͺ
and Simon is looking at my oximeter reͺͺͺ

"Eighty-five percent," I hear him tell Seraphina. After aͺ ͺͺͺ
pre-climb research, I know that this is not ideal. Though it can vary,
anything under ninety is never ideal.

*Oh, no. Acute mountain sickness. Decreased levels of oxygen at high alti-
tudes. Insufficient time for your body to adjust.*

I've read about it a million times. At best, I'd need to descend to a
lower altitude immediately and miss out on the opportunity to finish
the climb. At worst, I'd develop something like high-altitude cerebral
edema—swelling in the brain tissue due to buildup of fluid in the cra-
nium. I think of the symptoms. Severe headaches, hallucination, loss
of consciousness, disorientation, loss of coordination, memory loss,
coma. They tend to set in at night.

I remember that it's lunchtime. Maybe I'm okay after all. I begin
to feel better.

"That's good. We just need to keep an eye on her. Is she respon-
sive now?"

I can hear the conversation going on all around me.

"Marren?" Chris says.

"Yes?" I manage.

"She can talk now," he says.

Seraphina comes over to me and kneels. "Marren, are you feeling better? Do you have a headache? Shortness of breath? Do you know where we are?"

Chris lifts me to a sitting position, and I turn to Seraphina, who is assessing me with her powerful eyes. Leslie offers me a damp cloth to place on my forehead. I can hear her saying that it's all going to be okay.

"We're climbing Mount Kilimanjaro," I say. "This is—" I pause to look around, trying to remember. "This is the Shira 2 Camp. We stopped to have lunch here."

A giant smile breaks out across Seraphina's face. She looks at Leslie, who is studying me like a concerned mother.

"You're gonna be just fine, Marren," I hear Leslie say, her voice full of syrupy-sweet encouragement.

At Chris's urging, I take a long drink from my water bottle. My headache begins to subside. I feel energy returning. My breathing stabilizes, and I begin to tell myself that I just panicked. My incessant research about everything that can go wrong on a mountain climb has caught up with me. I know the symptoms of altitude sickness, both minor and severe, like the back of my hand. When Simon pointed out the emergency evacuation route, pulled out the oximeter, and reminded us that this was the first point where climbers usually began to feel sick, some sort of panic attack must have taken over.

I look at Chris, suddenly embarrassed.

"I feel much better now," I say. "Guess I must be a little dehydrated. Thank you," I say to Seraphina.

She smiles and everyone returns to lunch. The debacle soon fades into the background, and we return to the trail. Though Simon and

Chris still appear concerned, I no longer am. I feel better than ever, ready to forge ahead. *Panic attacks and dehydration, beware. You will not keep me from this goal of mine.*

Our journey continues. The terrain gets a bit rockier, with a growing paucity of vegetation. Occasionally, we pass rocks doused in orange and green—the color of lichens that are growing on top of them—but most of the rocks we see are a dull gray. Eventually, we stop at a lava bluff where Simon points out Cape buffalo tracks. He explains that buffalo will actually climb to this altitude to find salt licks in caves, where they can get essential nutrients. I am intrigued.

tion with me.

An icy wind greets us as we arrive at Moir Camp, which sits at the end of a large gorge that resembles the inside of a giant gray basin. In the distance is a weathered white teepee, something that Simon tells us was formerly used for research and sometimes as a hiding place for poachers. Thanks to our porters, a sea of orange and gray tents (with one distinctively red one in the mix) awaits us as we prepare for another night on the mountain.

At the precise moment that I reach Old Red, Chris calls to me, camera in hand again.

"Marren," he says. "Come here." He nods toward himself. "I want to show you something."

I turn to him and answer his call, like a little lost puppy.

When I reach him, he hands me his camera.

"Here, I want you to hold this," he says.

My fingers fumble around, like I'm a new parent finagling a tiny infant. I have no idea what I'm doing. Photography has never been a talent of mine. The word "Nikon" jumps out at me, a restless stranger in my arms.

Chris cradles my hands in his, steadying my grip. "Use both hands," he says. "Hold the right side of the camera with your right hand and support the lens with your left. Keep the camera as close as possible to your body so that it is still."

He moves his hands over mine, and my insides tingle. An orange-red sun appears in the distance.

"Ah," Chris says, taking the camera from me for a moment. "A perfect opportunity. I'm just going to adjust the aperture—the opening in the lens that controls the light—so that it is smaller. Narrow apertures are best for landscape shots like this. Now, you try. Take some shots."

He returns the camera to me, and I practice the hold he has demonstrated. I press the button at the top, and I hear the sound of pictures being taken. After I've attempted a few, I hand the camera back to him, and he studies what I've done.

"Very nice, Marren," he says. "Did you know that photography uncovers truth?"

What?

I furrow my brow, unsure of what he means.

"The great photographer Ansel Adams once said that to photograph truthfully and effectively is to see beneath the surfaces. And isn't anything beneath the surface laced with reality?"

I guess it is.

His eyes meet mine, and they hold my gaze.

Despite what I've been through, I am taken with this man, someone who is patient and willing to instruct me here on a mountain in Africa, who seeks to see things on a level much deeper than they appear.

20

It's combined with

buds are so impressed by this simple combination. Perhaps I'm just exhausted, grateful to have made it this far, thankful for the chance to eat anything at all right now. Whatever the reason, I feel as if I'm dining in a five-star restaurant with wonderful friends.

I look around the table, noticing every member of our group with gratitude now. Seraphina and her take-charge attitude, Leslie and her innate kindness, Casey and Claire and the way they lighten the mood—always making things a little more tolerable and fun. And of course, there is Chris, with whom I have found a special chemistry. Nothing romantic yet, but something comfortable. Easy. I wonder where this chemistry between us will go. For now, it's going up a mountain. Where that will lead, no one knows.

After dinner, the intense cold deters no one. Some of the porters and other crew members, decked out in full parkas and balaclavas, throw Frisbees and listen to music. The rest of us gather around a large campfire, our bundled bodies like dark puffy mounds, hovering together as we listen to Simon tell some of the most interesting stories I've ever heard—Swahili folktales that he promised would not disappoint.

Tonight he relates the story of Hasnaa—a female African lion cub who was mistreated by the other cubs in her pride because she was very beautiful. Hasnaa means "beautiful" in Swahili, Simon tells us as he continues. Little Hasnaa is excluded and lonely, and one day she goes out exploring on her own. She encounters a mouse who looks tasty. Killing the mouse would make her feel worthwhile, she thinks, because if she could successfully hunt alone, the others would surely be impressed. She'd bring the mouse back to show them, and they would respect her. But as Hasnaa corners the mouse, the tiny creature begs for his life, saying that he cannot leave his orphaned sister alone. Hasnaa cannot go through with it. She returns to the pride and continues to be bullied. One day, two orphaned young lions—one male and one female—wander into the pride, needing a group to join. The young male lion befriends Hasnaa and is nice to her. He protects her. And one night, as they are talking, he tells her that he is actually the mouse that she chose not to kill and his sister is the orphaned one that he couldn't bear to leave. He is grateful to her for her compassion. They become best friends and live happily ever after in the pride. He makes sure that she is never mistreated again.

Simon speaks with vigor and passion, in a way that tells me how much he loves to tell stories. How much he loves this grueling job of his. Though he is only twenty-eight years old, I'm certain that Simon has many of his own stories to tell, that he has probably lived one of the most fulfilling lives of us all.

The wind whips fiercely, making conditions intolerable for me. The others seem content, willing to stay and hear Simon tell a few additional tales, apparently unfazed by these frigid temperatures. I, however, am extremely disturbed by the fact that I can no longer feel my fingers or toes, so I decide that it's time for me to go. I seek shelter in my tent, and Chris asks to join me. I say yes. The others don't seem to care, although I do see a rather interesting look on Claire's face when we leave the campfire circle together. If her look was translated into a written word, it would read, "Inappropriate!" Chris and I say goodnight to everyone, and the others reciprocate.

Butterflies flitter in my stomach as I wonder where this is going. It almost feels sordid, the two of us heading back to my tent together. Like we're heading to some semi-private hotel room that's not

done this before—the talking-inside-

gloves, the fun g

able to see his nighttime hazel-green eyes and his plump, chapped lips, I am taken again by his rugged good looks. He laughs at me as I snuggle into my sleeping bag for extra warmth. I feel like a caterpillar in a cocoon, and I am hoping that whatever words we exchange will free me into a beautiful new butterfly with bright wings.

"Do you want to talk about the accident?" he says.

I flash back to the day after I turned eighteen. How one minute, I was sitting on the couch watching a late-night movie with my high school boyfriend. How the next, his mother would answer the doorbell, only to find two police officers, friends of Brody's family and mine in the Clear Springs community where we lived, each of them wearing a somber look, both woefully unprepared to deliver such horrible news.

My parents were dead.

Rich and Pat Lowery. Good people. Gone too soon. All because of Sadie Heard, the sixteen-year-old daughter of Stu and LeAnne

Heard, owners of Heard's Hardware, a staple on the Clear Springs town square.

Sadie was a nice girl—smart and hardworking, loved by most everyone in Clear Springs. She'd spent many a summer helping out at her parents' store, and I guess you could say that she was somewhat famous around town. Sweet Sadie. From her toddler years to her teenage ones, seeing Sadie running around Heard's had always been one of the more pleasant parts of small-town life. Her smile was infectious.

Sadie had gotten her driver's license just a month before the accident. Apparently, she was looking down at her Blackberry as she drove through the light at Cedar Avenue and First Street and broadsided my father's vintage convertible Mustang—one of his prized possessions—on that now infamous Saturday evening.

Seeing Sadie for the first time after the accident was something I'll never forget. She was hysterical, the words "I'm so sorry" spewing repeatedly from her mouth like a broken record. Her eyes were swollen shut from what appeared to be hours of crying. When I looked at her, I didn't feel fury. I felt sorrow. This poor girl was going to have to live with the consequences of what she had done for the rest of her life, and nothing I could say or do was going to make it worse, or better.

Sadie had quickly gone from cheerleader and president of her sophomore class to the girl who killed Marren Lowery's parents. As bitter as I was, I just hugged her. She hadn't meant any harm. Poor thing. Six months later, she took her own life, and a month after that, Heard's hardware shut down for good. Stu and LeAnne moved away with their other two kids, and we never heard much about them again.

One moment of inattention had caused a lifetime of devastation. For everyone.

I don't want to talk about the death of my parents. I've had years to accept life after the accident, but only a few short months to cope with the fresh damage of losing Brody. It's Brody I need to discuss. But discussing Brody with Chris just seems wrong. Or does it?

I'm still freezing cold, but Chris's question warms me, lingering in my mind, inviting me to answer. I decide to tell him the truth, wondering if his response to my words will help to thaw the icy sting of my grief.

... talk about." I say, exhal-

assuage your pain and not ....

Should I be telling Chris this? Is he one of the *right* people? How do I know?

Chris looks at me with curious eyes. His concern seems genuine. Something about the way he is staring at me, waiting patiently for me to go on, tells me that he is safe. He is one of the right people. He will not squander my faith in him.

I close my eyes and take a deep breath, then I exhale slowly. The words jump to the tip of my tongue, and when I open my mouth, they dive right out of me.

"I haven't told you the truth," I say. I pause briefly. "The truth is that I lost my husband, Brody, to opioid addiction earlier this year. He was the love of my life, and the poison in those pills killed him long before the overdose did."

Chris's stare becomes wider, but his apparent concern fades. It's almost as if he understands what I'm saying. Like he's been there on some level. Our gazes connect, intertwining for a split second. The shame I felt when I first spoke the words magically disappears.

"I know, I know," I say. "I can't imagine what you must think of me now. Poor Marren, running away from an addict of a husband, expecting to find something she'll never find here on the world's tallest free-standing mountain. I'm crazy, right?"

He stares silently at me.

"I was thinking the opposite," he says. "About how brave it is of you to undertake something like this after what you've been through. I'm proud of you, Marren. You've nothing to be ashamed of."

Wow. For once, no judgment. No feeling that I have to defend or explain my life. Just pure, unadulterated support. I feel a smile coming on, followed by the need to shift the focus of our conversation to him.

"Now that I've told you my story, it's time for you to tell me yours. You said yourself that you're either running to or from something if you climb a mountain. So, tell me, Chris Courtland—what is it for you?"

"Oh, no," he says. "Tonight is all about *you*. Keep talking. I'm listening."

I draw in a breath.

21

flickers in the darkness outside distress. Uniformed personnel storm into our bedroom, where I am kneeling beside Brody, still frantically compressing.

"Please, wake up. Please, wake up."

An older man kneels next to me, but I cannot look at him. I have to bring Brody back to life.

"Ma'am, please. Let us try," the uniformed man says.

But I don't budge. I will not give up.

"Ma'am, please," the man says again. This time, another man and a woman gently grab my arms and lift me away from Brody.

"No!" I scream. "Let me go!"

But they are too strong for my fragile frame. I've been hollowed by the stress of hydrocodone. They carry me out to the front porch, where more uniformed responders are waiting. One places her arm around me, and I begin to sob. My face falls into her shoulder. She hands me my phone, which must have been beside me on the floor as I tried to save Brody.

A rush of adrenaline delivers the energy necessary for me to call George and Trish and beg them to come quickly. Before I know it, their black Mercedes screeches to a halt next to the curb. When I hear the sound of car doors smashing shut, I look up to see them, my eye still swollen and bruised from last night's incident. "Marren, sweetheart," Brody's father, George, says. "What on earth happened to you?"

I burst into tears. I cannot answer his question. Because it's not about what happened to me—it's about what happened to Brody.

A police officer approaches us and delivers the news: Brody is dead.

Brody is dead.

The officer is staring at me, concern brimming in his eyes. He is probably waiting for me to collapse, to fall into his arms screaming and crying out for help. Instead, I run back into the house, straight to our bedroom. But it is actually my bedroom now. Because Brody will never sleep here again. Ever.

I fumble through dresser drawers until I find some leggings, a sports bra, and an athletic top. I strip out of my sweater and jeans and throw on the workout attire, putting on sunglasses and grabbing my iPhone and some headphones before I run out the front door. I zoom past uniformed police officers and firefighters and my in-laws as I descend the front porch steps. People are staring at me, asking if I'm crazy. I don't pay any attention to them. I just keep running, for four whole miles in the forty-something-degree December air, up and down the streets of Clear Springs, listening to Lady A's "What if I Never Get Over You."

My affinity for running began after the accident. I couldn't escape my parents' death, but I could escape into the words of a song as I listened to it on a long, cathartic run. Sometimes, Brody would run with me. Those were some of our best days together— long before the pills. Now, he will never run with me again.

I pick up my pace. Run faster. Farther away from the pain of another loss I cannot bear. Sprinting the final stretch, I arrive back at the house, where George and Trish are waiting on the front porch. The look in George's eyes—seething and shocked under a pair of wire-rimmed glasses—demands an explanation.

"I'm sorry," I say, huffing, struggling to catch my breath. "But I had to."

Actually, I'm not sorry. I'm sweaty—but not sorry. Everyone reacts to death differently. Brody's baseball career died, and he took

. . . for a run. It's my kind of "differ-

Marren doesn't end up

will almost certainly jump right on this. And if anyone saw Marren running and snapped a pic, God forbid, the headline could be devastating. I can see it now, 'Local Baseball Phenom Dies, and His Wife Goes for a Run.'"

Trish places her head in her hands, and anger boils up inside of me.

Too bad I can't run away forever.

▲ ▲ ▲

Word of Brody's passing does travel fast. My phone explodes with text messages and calls. I eventually turn it off, because there is no way that I can field questions about the day's events right now. I feel the urge to run again, but I fend it off, because I know this might push my in-laws straight over the edge. They need me right now, and I need them too.

Trish is practically catatonic, slumped in a wingback chair that she picked out for our living room—now my living room—and I don't know what to say or do to help her. George is on the phone, talking to Mr. Weaver from the funeral home, and I am sitting alone in the kitchen, sipping some of Brody's vodka. This can't be happening.

After ending his phone conversation, George finds me in the kitchen and offers a hug. Numbed by the vodka, I lazily hug him back. We linger in our embrace, and I begin to cry. I haven't had enough vodka to curb my emotions completely.

"I knew it was bad," George says. "But I didn't know that it was this bad."

I sniffle as I sob.

"Did he do this to you?" George asks, tracing my eye gently with his fingers.

I don't want to, but I nod.

George bursts into tears, something that I've never seen him do. "God help us, Marren," he says. "What happened to the son I worked so hard to raise?"

22

forehead crinkled. Silence dances around us, flaunting its disturbing moves. My poisonous past has risen up to my tongue and begun to spew everywhere now. Toxicity lingers in the air.

"Wow," he says. "I don't know what to say. I'm so sorry . . . I wish I had the words."

Is that all he has to say? I'm not sure how to proceed with this shame that I've just shared, and Chris's lack of conversation isn't helping. I stare at him, suddenly mortified. Maybe he isn't the "right" person after all. But there's no going back now. I can't unsay what I've said. But I can say something else.

"That's it?" I blurt out.

He sits silently, clearly frazzled by my question.

"After everything I just told you, that's all you have to say to me?"

"Marren—"

"Just don't," I say, a wave of defensiveness crashing over me. I don't know where it's coming from. I haven't let anything like this surface in me for quite some time. "I guess I expected more from you."

What did I just say?

Clearly, I've caught him off guard. He inhales deeply and looks up at the sky as he purses his lips together. And then he says something I will never forget.

"Honestly, Marren, I really don't know what to say to you right now. But I'm glad you shared your pain with me," he says. "Because I think I can help to assuage it, if you'll just let me try."

He pats his shoulder and opens his arms, inviting me in. I fall into him as the agony of my past rears up in the form of loud, heart-wrenching sobs. He strokes the back of my head as I cry. I haven't cried like this in a very long time. Not since the funeral, in fact.

23

ominous sky above. A light ~~~~ ~~~
nity tears. Most of Clear Springs has assembled at the local United
Methodist church. Crowds of people spill over from the sanctuary
onto the sidewalks and into extra rooms inside the church building,
where the service is being livestreamed. I am amazed by the number
of attendees. The hidden drug habit that once alienated us from the
rest of our world has now brought everyone back together again.

Pitying stares and sympathetic nods are everywhere as George
escorts me to the front aisle. At first, I am seated alone—no children
or parents or brothers or sisters to share in my sorrow—but then a
minute later, Trish lands next to me. Her styled blond hair and put-
together presence is soothing, yet at the same time devastating. Our
combined loss is too much to bear: a talented son, a once-loving-yet-
abusive husband. She takes my hand as George sits next to her. We
are survivors, but today, we're more like victims.

The ceremony begins. Touching words from family and
friends do little to console me. I am, however, moved by a striking

rendition of "It Is Well with My Soul"—its poignant words resonating through the air, floating on the coattails of shrieking organ
pipes. The powerful notes pierce my composure as I remember
this same song being played at my parents' funeral. Still, I remain
vigilant: tear free, stoic, and strong in an ocean of heartbreak.
That's one thing my grandmother taught me: no one wants to witness hysteria at a funeral. Just like everything else about a good
Southern lady, mourning is supposed to be classy. I am therefore
determined to be devastated yet composed.

Later, after an unpleasant ride into the wooded depths of rural
Arkansas, we bury Brody in the Old Kingston Cemetery, about five
miles outside of town. Generations of Hallecks are buried here—
German immigrants who once found their way to the United States
long, long ago. Brody once told me about his father's obsession with
ancestry. He taught Brody all about the great influx of Germans
into the United States in the 1800s—some of them, including
George's great-grandfather, were recruited to help construct the
Little Rock and Fort Smith Railroad in the late 1870s. A handful
of these German railroad workers and their families settled in and
around Clear Springs, and many were laid to rest here at the Old
Kingston Cemetery. A twinge of agony enters my stomach as I realize that Brody will soon be among them.

The interment is private. A small group of friends and family hud-
dle together under a large white tent that provides shelter from the
rain, which has intensified now. I begin to think of today as Black
Thursday, because darkness is everywhere—in my mind, in the sky
above me, and on the bodies of the people surrounding me. Everyone
here is wearing black, another unwritten Southern rule. Any good
Southerner wouldn't dare show up to a funeral wearing any other
color. It is the only way to show proper sympathy and respect.

Black Thursday continues its grueling course as our local pastor,
Dr. John Frye, speaks the final words about Brody's life. I focus on

the spray of red roses that rests atop Brody's casket, my expression hidden behind large, black, Jackie O–type sunglasses. In spite of the rain, which is beating hard against the tent now like some sort of rapid drumbeat, these sunglasses are still necessary. They block the guests' ability to see my eyes, to see inside my pain.

It finally stops raining as the interment comes to an end. The people begin to scatter, most of them having no idea what to say or do. Amidst awkward hugs are soft whispers of "We're praying for you, Marren," and "We're so sorry for you, Marren," and "Sending … Marren." Though well-

nize those long, slender legs and …

What is she doing here?

She is Colette McSwain—daughter of Collin McSwain, former mayor of Clear Springs and heir to the McSwain family dynasty of chicken farms. Some nerve Colette has, daring to show up at Brody's interment after the hell she put me through. I study her profile as she prances behind her mother Yvette, a former cocktail waitress that Collin apparently met on a trip to Vegas and somehow convinced to move to small-town Arkansas. The mother-and-daughter duo walk together, their matching tresses framing identical heart-shaped faces, which are covered by similar dark sunglasses, until they reach the Range Rover that everyone knew Collin was bound to purchase someday. I watch him smooth his salt-and-pepper hair in the side mirror as he ushers his wife and daughter into the car and they climb in.

My composure is paper thin now. I suddenly want to run after Colette, to pluck her from her chariot and throw her straight to the ground. To pull every lock of that hair from her head and strangle her, to hit her so hard that she feels half as bad as I did on the day I discovered what was going on between her and Brody.

About six months after Brody's injury, I finally realized that he had a problem. Until then, I'd chalked every abnormality up to the surgery, every strange new occurrence up to his rehabilitation process. Four to six months, the doctor had said. That's how long I expected it would take for him to make a full recovery. Naively, I'd just assumed that at the end of this period, everything would go back to normal.

But it didn't.

Slowly and painfully, our "normal" deteriorated into something completely unrecognizable. I couldn't carry on a regular conversation with Brody—at times he just didn't make sense. His demeanor slowed greatly, and occasionally, he would bump into the wall or stumble as he walked around. Obviously unable to play baseball or pursue any other type of career, he became incapable of doing much of anything at all. He couldn't help around the house. Couldn't help buy the groceries, fold the laundry, or cook anything for himself. Sometimes, he'd beg me for the car keys so he could go for a drive, and immediately I felt like I was in Vegas, contemplating a game of Russian roulette—allowing him to drive under the influence of hydrocodone a gamble I knew I shouldn't take. But oh, those eyes when he begged me. So beautiful and pitiful at the same time. They held a strange power over me, forcing me to do things I shouldn't.

I often thought about confronting George and Trish about his concerning behavior, but I didn't want to upset them. They were already devastated enough by the fact that their son's potential to play major league baseball had been all but destroyed by an unforeseen injury.

So I confronted Brody instead.

"You have a problem," I said. "And I think we need to get you some help."

Tears—from my eyes and his—ensued. It was as if I'd uncovered a hidden virus, allowing the sunlight to expose and slowly begin to try and destroy it. I held his head in my hands as he cried like a baby, clearly terrified of the road ahead and whatever it might bring.

"I'll get some help, Marren," he said. "I promise you. I'll go to meetings and get a sponsor. I will get better." And I believed him.

I would later discover that the "meetings" he claimed to be and the "sponsor"

Clear Springs had likely assumed been somewhat jealous of Colette's good looks and her power over men. Of her past relationship with my husband. If only Brody hadn't blundered one night during what was likely a pill-induced high, telling me that his "meetings" were at the hotel, I might never have known about their sordid reconciliation. Sadly, he probably didn't even remember telling me.

Every Thursday night, he'd venture out to one of his "meetings," and I prayed hard that things would soon improve. But when they didn't, and the signs that he was taking pills became apparent again, I became suspicious. The meetings obviously weren't working, and the sponsor obviously wasn't convincing him not to use. I knew I had to step in and do something.

Instead of confronting him directly, I played my cards more carefully, and I decided to secretly follow him to one of his weekly "meetings." At first, I was pleased to see that he hadn't lied about where he was going. He did, in fact, go to the hotel that he'd said he'd been going to. But the truth ended there.

I can't explain the rage I experienced when I first saw Brody together with Colette in the hotel lobby, the feeling that ravaged me as they embraced. But just as I was about to step in and ruin their rendezvous, they parted ways, and I questioned my jealousy. She went one way, and he went another. Perhaps it was coincidence, the two of them running into each other unexpectedly at a hotel and greeting each other a little too affectionately.

After Colette disappeared, I waited for Brody to make his way to a conference room, hoping he would actually do what he promised me he was doing. Instead, he made his way to a nearby elevator. He went up and never came down. Two minutes later, Colette emerged from the lobby bar, with her perfect blond beach waves hovering over a bottle of champagne. She also got on the elevator. It didn't take a genius to figure out what was going on.

Three hours later, I sat in the hotel lobby, glued to my iPhone, waiting to catch one of them on the way down. Finally, Colette stepped into view, looking much more tattered than before. Never had I seen her with such disheveled hair, with such wrinkled clothing. Her walk was part strut and part stumble. I made my way toward her, and she stumbled straight into me.

"Marren!" she said, obviously shocked. "What are you doing here?"

"Oh, I don't know, Colette. I could ask you the same question."

As she stood, frozen and staring at me, her eyes full of shame, I caught a glimpse of Brody, unsteadily making his way to the front exit toward simple automatic double doors.

"Brody!" I shouted.

He immediately stopped and turned around. Seeing me and Colette standing there together sent him into a wide-eyed panic, and he immediately bolted out the door.

Colette hurried away, chasing after him.

After that, he stopped going to "meetings" and talking to his "sponsor." I contemplated leaving him back then, but he begged so pathetically for forgiveness that I was forced to stay. Brody's drug addiction had driven my heart into a wall, and the sight of him with Colette had ripped my soul from my body. I was terrified—a heartless, soulless sham of a young woman wondering what in the hell I was going to do.

Strangely enough, I am feeling exactly the same way now. I

_ _ _ _ and live the life

anger transforms to jealousy, because

They have each other, and I have no one, nothing but grief and regret. I am clearly unprepared for the anguish to come.

24

WHEN I FINISH THE REST of the story, tears are streaming down my swollen red cheeks. Chris continues to cradle me in his arms, and they feel strong, like a safety net that has just caught me after a freefall. Like the net, Chris is rugged and durable on the outside, and the way that he is holding me now suggests that he's protective on the inside, too.

He takes a finger and swipes a glob of clear liquid from my face.

"It's all right, Marren. I'm here." His words greet me like a hug from a best friend—a champion listener and faithful supporter.

I cry harder, unable to believe that I've shared so much of myself with this total stranger. But though he is a stranger, something about him feels very familiar. Like we could have been high school besties—in the same way that Brody and I once were.

I regain my composure, and I dare to continue.

"There's something else I have to tell you," I say, sniffling. When I say the words, Chris's eyes widen. He immediately sits up, as if I've conjured some sort of strange rush of adrenaline inside of him.

25

than the stress or living with ....

The steady flow of cards, texts, calls, and casseroles from people in the community cannot erase my pain, but it does lift my spirits in tiny little ways. I make sure to write a thank-you note to each and every person who sends something, because in spite of everything that has happened, I want to be considered a classy Southern lady.

Every Southern woman should know how to send a thank-you note, my grandmother once told me. Gratitude is a must when it comes to good manners.

They say that trying times show you who a person really is. In my time of trouble, I want to have good manners. I want to make my grandmother proud, to show the world that she helped raise a good person. I wish I felt like a good person. I wish I felt anything good at all.

George and Trish have been seeing a grief counselor named Greta. In the first month after Brody's death, Trish couldn't leave the house. She was so devastated that she literally stayed in bed for an entire month. By the end of month two, she was drinking every day. All day, sometimes. One afternoon she drove over to my house, day-drunk and screaming that I should have done more to help Brody, that his death was all my fault. I cried. She cried too. It was a devastating mess. That's when George insisted that she get some help. He would go too. Trish apologized to me, and I forgave her. Grief is a monster, and it will rear its head in the ugliest of ways sometimes.

George and Trish see Greta every Tuesday at eleven in the morning, just before they come over to my house for lunch. This past Tuesday, Trish begged me to see Greta too.

"You're wasting away, Marren. I'm worried sick about you. Brody wouldn't want this," Trish says. "Please come with us. You'll love her."

But I refuse. I don't want to talk about this anymore. I just want it all to go away, to leave me alone for good.

Trish and George leave me with Greta's card anyway. Once they are gone, I pick it up and stare at it. Greta's number stares back at me longingly, in bold black font. There is a small part of me that wants to dial it, and yet I do not. Instead, I pull out a Diet Coke and I pop it open before I sit down to do some writing—something I haven't done much of lately. At least not after the fight.

It started one night when Brody mentioned our annual dinner with his former baseball teammates and their wives. Even after Brody's injury, we gathered every year at a restaurant in Little Rock to celebrate our friendships. We'd made some wonderful friends through baseball before the pills came into the picture, and the annual dinner was an opportunity to keep those friendships alive.

"So they planned the annual dinner at Brave New Restaurant for Saturday, May 6th," Brody informed me. "Mark your calendar."

Oh, no. Saturday, May 6th?

"Brody, I—" My hands began to shake. Missing the annual dinner wasn't an option. How could I possibly tell him?

"You what?"

"I signed up for a writing conference that weekend. It's my very first one. I was going to drive to Memphis and stay the night with Mr. and Mrs. Sherman—remember my mom's best friend from college? I haven't seen her in ages—"

"You'll have to cancel it," he said.

"But—"

the annual dinner. You

"All right. I'll cancel it,

my mouth.

"Good," he said, taking a sip from his glass.

After that, I quit writing for a long time. What good was it going to do? He'd never support it.

Maybe I do need to talk to Greta. Or maybe I can just write the pain away now. I start typing on the computer, and it feels good.

Later that evening, George and Trish return. They've brought me dinner, a grilled chicken salad from the Terracotta Café. This makes me smile. I am happy to have company. It's never fun to eat alone.

After dinner, George helps Trish clean the kitchen as I sit at the table with my laptop. They insist that I relax. I watch as they wipe things down and run the silverware under the faucet and load the dishwasher. They are a great team. *Brody and I will never be a team again*, I think. I look at my laptop, searching for a distraction.

"Marren, there's something we want to talk to you about," he says, loading the final dish into the dishwasher.

He walks toward me and takes a seat at the table. I can see a pensive expression form across his face, one that Brody always referred to as "the look." Whenever George gets the look, something earthshaking usually follows. I brace myself, like a passenger on a flight that is about to crash land.

"Trish and I have decided to file a lawsuit against Frasier Industries—the pharmaceutical company that made and distributed the hydrocodone."

The *hydrocodone*. That word again. Just hearing it feels like a punch to my gut. George brings a hand to his temple as he sighs loudly. There is pain in the sound that comes out of him. He has clearly been gut punched too.

"We've hired a lawyer in Little Rock. We're going up to meet with her next week. Her name is Tara Rowe. She's at Behring, Davis, and Coburn—one of the bigger plaintiffs' firms up there. A friend of a friend. They say she's the best. A wolf in sheep's clothing."

My mind wanders like a lost child. George's look finds me again, collects me, and brings me home, reminding me that I cannot escape. This is where I must continue to live. I must do as I'm told.

"If we win, the money will go to the new foundation that we intend to establish in Brody's honor," George says.

I widen my eyes. Money? Foundation?

"Why didn't you tell me about all of this?" I ask.

"We should have, but everything has just been so hard lately. We wanted to give it some time. We wanted to give you some time."

I want to tell them that all the time in the world wouldn't make me want to participate in something like this, but I can't. I hate the feeling that is slowly overtaking me. It's the same feeling I had when I watched Brody with his pills. I am a dog in a cage, controlled by my owner. Powerless.

Trish smiles and pats my arm. "We'd love for you to come with us to meet with Tara," she says. Her scarlet lipstick glistens as a smile spreads slowly across her face. "And I'd also love it if you'd serve on the board of the new foundation. We can fight this together. We can use Brody's legacy to help others. I know that's what he would want."

My heart sinks and swells at the same time. On one hand, I want ʰ⁺ to live on, but on the other hand, I don't. A lawsuit will dig ⁻ⁱᵉᵈ deep inside of me, ones I don't want to ⁻ᵗⁱⁿᵘᵉˢ to inhabit George's that isn't

Tara Rowe is a striking woman. Her glowing, and crystal green eyes are a unique combination. She seems more supermodel than super-lawyer. Still, her legal track record is impeccable. She's just been voted Arkansas litigator of the year, and she is the president-elect of the Arkansas Bar Association and a gifted speaker whose demeanor is very presidential (I watched her give a presentation in a YouTube video). I am extremely impressed with Tara. If anyone is going to lead us effectively in the fight against Frasier Industries, she's the one.

We gather in a corner conference room, and Tara takes a seat across from me, George, and Trish. She is dressed in a conservative navy suit with a cream-colored blouse. Her tiny pearl earrings exude professionalism, as does her leather notepad holder and fancy black pen.

"So tell me," Tara says. "Why exactly do you want to do this?"

George looks at Trish, and Trish chews on her lower lip. I sit quietly between them, unable to render an answer.

"Our son was a good man," George finally says. "And then he wasn't. All because of some vile little pills that he never should have been given. We want to send the message that these things can destroy people. The public deserves to know the full story, to know that the choice to prescribe these things and the choice to take them have potentially lethal consequences. Someone at Frasier Industries clearly knew about this and didn't disclose."

I can't help but nod as Tara scribbles on her legal pad.

"I see," she says, just before she looks up from her pad. "And I'd love to help you with that. But before we move forward, I want to make it clear that litigation of this sort can stir up a lot of pain. I feel the need to let you know that tall-building lawyers who represent Big Pharma can paint Brody into a monster. You can be dragged through the mud emotionally—be made to feel guilt you should never have to feel. I don't mean to discourage you. I just want you to know what you're up against. These kind of lawsuits . . . they're never easy, and frankly, they're almost impossible to win. But fighting a force that is much greater than you are is never easy, is it, even if the cause is noble."

I shake my head. At least she is honest.

"Ms. Rowe," Trish begins, in her most polite tone, "I want to know that I did everything in my power to save others from the fate of my son. If I can die knowing that I did all I could, then everything will be worth it, even if we lose."

"Well then," she says. "Let's move forward, shall we? I'll have my assistant email you an engagement letter, which you can sign and return at your earliest convenience. When I receive it, I'll have one of my associates draft a memo on potential claims we can bring against Frasier Industries. We'll discuss these and go from there."

I manage a hesitant smile. George and Trish nod in agreement.

"Any other questions for now?" Tara asks.

I raise my hand slightly.

"Will I have to testify?" I ask. "Because I'm not sure if I'm ready for that yet."

Tara looks me in the eye. Her calm, presidential presence reassures me once again.

"When the time comes for you to share your story," she says, "I promise that I will make you ready."

▲ ▲ ▲

you in the case of *Halleck v. Frasier Industries*." His deep voice resonates throughout the room. "I'd like to begin by asking you to describe your late husband's first encounter with pills."

I can't.

"Can you tell me about the night of his death? Do you recall exactly what happened?"

I won't. It's too much.

"Mrs. Halleck? I need you to tell me what happened that night."

The pain boils up inside of me and overflows, jarring the lid from the heated pot of my emotions. I leap from my chair and bolt out of the conference room. Suddenly, I am in the wilderness, and Brody is with me, carrying a machete. He is pre-drug-addiction handsome, his sandy-blond hair falling over into his emerald eyes. We are hiking through a mess of overgrowth, tangles of thick vegetation everywhere around us, preventing us from getting anywhere.

We fight our way through, Brody and his machete paving the path forward, and then we come to a place that makes us turn to look at each other in despair.

Ahead of us is a mountain, land so formidable that we're sure we can't continue. Brody turns to look at me and says this: "I know you can do this, Mare. I know you can. You can get over this mountain." And then he hands me the machete and disappears.

26

way. The inflection sounds like fear and reeks of concern.

"What's wrong?" I ask. This was not the response I expected.

"So you're suing Frasier Industries?" he asks.

I nod.

He closes his eyes and draws in a breath. When he exhales, he sits silently. Something is definitely off.

"Marren, there's something *I* need to tell *you*," he says.

His lips have barely parted when we hear Casey's harrowing cry for help.

"Claire! Please, someone help us!"

Chris springs from my tent to see what's happening, and I follow.

We look over at the campfire, where Claire is hunched over, a bundled mess, saying she can't breathe, clutching her chest. Simon is measuring her oxygen levels with the oximeter, and the look on his face when he stares down at the results says it all. He doesn't have to say it out loud, although he does.

"Sixty-five percent," he says, frowning.

"Here, let me listen to your lungs," I hear Seraphina say. Leslie is running toward Claire, holding a stethoscope that she and Seraphina must have brought with them on the trip.

Simon's fingers move swiftly across the buttons of his satellite phone. He yells out something in Swahili that I don't understand, and porters and crew members emerge from everywhere.

"We need to get her down to lower altitude. I will arrange for help to meet you at the emergency evacuation route at Shira 2." His voice is stern, void of panic, but full of urgency.

I am close enough to the chaos now that I can see Claire's lips peering out from under her balaclava. They are an eerie shade of blue-gray. Her breathing sounds funny, marred by a strange rattling. One of the porters grabs a portable stretcher and brings it over toward her. Seraphina burrows through Claire's layers of clothing to listen to her chest.

"She needs to be hospitalized as soon as possible," says Seraphina as she removes the earbuds of her stethoscope. "I don't like the crackling sounds I'm hearing. She needs to descend immediately and be seen by a physician."

Crackling sounds. Oh, no. Yet another type of acute mountain sickness. I immediately think of an article I recently read on high-altitude pulmonary edema—a condition that causes excess fluid on the lungs due to oxygen deprivation at high altitudes. The article mentioned that crackling sounds can be heard when listening to the lungs. If not treated immediately, the condition can be deadly. The cure, as Seraphina has suggested, is to immediately descend to lower altitude.

Leslie takes Claire's hand and tells her that everything is going to be just fine. Seraphina turns to Casey. "She's gonna make it through this," Seraphina says. "And I want you to promise me that you'll remain calm so that you can take care of her."

Casey nods. The once carefree look in his eyes has turned serious. He holds Claire's hand and strokes it gently, softly repeating, "I love you, and you're going to be okay."

The porters load Claire on the stretcher, armed with headlamps, and whisk her away to lower ground. Casey follows behind, and we are all left defeated. We look to Simon, who inspires us a little.

"She is in good hands," he says. "I trust that she will be fine. *Safari lazima iendelee!*"

We stare at Simon. Even Seraphina looks confused.

The night is torture, like a cold shower in darkness that lasts for several hours. When I finally do get to sleep, it is only a half-sleep, and I end up dreaming of Brody. My dream takes me back to the time when he took me camping in the fall on the Buffalo River in Arkansas.

Fall in Arkansas is sublime—autumn reds, greens, and golds are draped everywhere. Days are temperate, perfectly conducive to hiking down trails or canoeing down a calm river, but nights are sometimes brutal, falling into the lower forties or below. In my dream, I recall how Brody and I glided down the river in our canoe that day, absorbing the high bluffs and changing colors all around us as the sun propelled us with its seventy-five-degree warmth. That night, however, the temperature plummeted to almost thirty degrees, and I was left suffering with a flimsy sleeping bag that did little to rescue me. Not even Brody's strong arms and warming touch could remedy my aversion to the cold. I hated it, and I swore I'd never do anything like it again—a promise to myself that I've now clearly broken. I am excruciatingly cold, inside and out, scared of hypothermia—perhaps even more terrified that my grief will never completely thaw.

At six in the morning, I wake to yet another frost-covered tent, hardly prepared for another long day and night that I assume will only get colder. I attempt to read some Hemingway, but my copy of "The Snows of Kilimanjaro" flies out of my hands when I'm startled by someone rapping on the outside of Old Red.

"Rise and shine, sleepyhead," the voice says. "Time for breakfast."

I recognize the sexy scruff of his tone. It's Chris. I suddenly wonder why he is outside of my tent this early, apparently anxious for me to come out. Part of me is annoyed, like he is interrupting the serenity of my morning. The other part of me is flattered by the fact that he cares enough to personally stop by and invite me to begin the day with him. Shouldn't I be ecstatic that the handsome cowboy from Texas is here now, talking to me?

"I'm coming," I say.

▲ ▲ ▲

When I arrive at the dining tent, Chris is standing outside. I wonder if he's waiting for me. I also wonder what he was going to say just before the awful incident with Claire last night.

"So, what is it that you were going to tell me?" I ask. It's been bothering me all night. I can no longer stand the suspense.

He looks at me with those magnetic eyes, and then he purses his lips, like he's hesitating.

"Marren, I hope you don't mind me asking you this," Chris says. "But I'm curious about something."

We walk in together, making our way toward the coffee, and I wait for him to continue.

"Why are you here right now?" he says, grabbing a cup.

I tilt my head in confusion as I watch him dispense the coffee into the cup.

"Are you here for *you*, or are you here for *him*? Because from everything you've told me, it sure sounds like you're still doing everything for him. And for the life of me, I don't understand why."

I narrow my eyes at Chris. How dare he make such a patronizing

ɑest to survive here, and he has

you re giving ɪ

for the strong woman you are. You don't have to hide behind your shame anymore. If I were you, I'd convince his parents to drop the lawsuit. Because it's no longer about *him*. It's about you moving on with *your* life."

His words sting, and yet they ring beautifully within me.

Before I can respond, Simon gathers us for our daily briefing. "Claire has made it to a local hospital," he says, "and she is going to be just fine. I have spoken to Casey, and he's still shaken up but will be fine too."

We break out into collective applause, celebrating the news. Still, I feel a bit deflated. Casey and Claire were part of our adventure, and now they are missing. Their fresh young faces and unique attempts at humor (like the "Kili Me Softly" T-shirts) are missing too.

"Will they be able to return?" I ask. "Maybe join us somewhere at one of our next campsites?"

Simon shakes his head. "I am very sorry, Marren," he says, "but I am afraid not."

"I guess it's survival of the fittest up here," Chris says. "Maybe they should have trained a little harder."

A wave of shock travels through me. How can he be so attractive and insensitive at the same time?

"Take that back," I say.

"What?" Chris says.

"You heard me. That was rude. It's not their fault. They didn't do anything to cause Claire's sickness." I think back to the times with Brody and his addiction, to the fear of people finding out and blaming me for his demise.

It's not my fault. I didn't cause it. And how dare anyone insinuate that I did.

I get my own coffee and walk away from Chris. He's mumbling some sort of apology, but I hardly have the patience for it right now.

27

Simon explains.

will eventually reach the Lava Tower, where we will eat lunch. Thereafter, we will descend to our campsite at Barranco Camp."

The alpine desert looks something like a faraway planet, something like Jupiter, distinguished by a yellow-gray-green mixture of volcanic leftovers. Years ago, I knew Jupiter very well, because I'd done an eighth-grade presentation on it. Though time has muddied the details, some of them are still legible in my mind, permanently etched into my brain.

Interesting facts about Jupiter: it has the shortest day of all the planets, at least 67 moons, and thick cloud layers made of ammonia crystals and sulfur . . .

I remember typing up the full report and presenting it to the class, along with a detailed Styrofoam model, painted in the same hues that surround me right now. It occurs to me that this trip to Kilimanjaro has conjured the same type of curiosity from me that the Jupiter assignment once elicited. For the first time in a long time,

I am genuinely interested in learning about a faraway place and all of its interesting facts.

Our progression to this new biome has left me curious. Plants and trees are extremely scarce now, and any kind of wildlife would surely struggle to survive in such desolate conditions. Still, we are able to find more Cape buffalo tracks, which Simon explains are caused by pure desperation—animals who are struggling to find nutrients somewhere, even soil at amazingly high altitudes.

I adjust my balaclava, a bandana-like face covering that has become a necessity now. The wind is so cold, so bitter and biting that I'm certain my face will freeze soon. I think back to the story of Beck Weathers, a Dallas pathologist who attempted to summit Mount Everest in the true story that is told in the famous nonfiction book-turned-movie *Into Thin Air.* I picture Beck's frostbitten nose and cheeks, black and hard to look at, after he was mistaken as dead during an unexpected snowstorm. Though he survived, and his facial features were eventually reconstructed, I'm fairly certain I don't have the resilience of Beck Weathers.

Please, God, don't let my face freeze.

Chris appears beside me, with his balaclava in full force too, and we stare at each other like thieves, our faces hidden from view. The wind is excruciating, but the view of Mount Meru in the distance is gratifying. Its summit stands solemnly above cottony wisps of clouds, staring back at us from almost seventy kilometers away.

Mount Meru is the fifth-highest mountain in Africa, Simon tells us, and the second highest in Tanzania. I'm thankful for a glimpse of its distant beauty, for I miss the alluring vegetation that we so frequently saw in the rainforest, heath, and moorlands. The only interesting site here is that of more buffalo tracks, along with the disturbing presence of decaying buffalo bones not too far away from the trail. It's almost like watching a movie in full color and then having it suddenly change into black and white: still a great show, yet not quite as satisfying.

"Hey, go stand over there," Chris says, pointing to a scenic spot with Mount Meru in the background. "I want a picture."

"Of me?" I say, my teeth chattering.

He nods as he messes with the buttons on his camera.

"But it's so cold. And I look like the Stay-Puft Marshmallow Woman wearing a bank robber's mask." I can barely speak the words now. My lips are frozen, even in the shelter of my balaclava.

"Just get over there," he says. "Now, pretend like you're on the beach somewhere, soaking up the ninety-five-degree sun with a piña

The wind eventually dies down, and the chill in the air becomes tolerable. Chris snaps more pictures as we come to the Lava Tower—a large column of rocks that reminds me of a black-and-orange Jabba the Hutt from *Star Wars*. It is tall and wide and worthy of my attention, a unique sight along an otherwise uneventful day's journey. A thick sea of white lurks beneath us, and for the first time, I realize that we are above the clouds.

Simon recommends that we have lunch here at Lava Tower and says that a trip to the top will help us to acclimatize and offer breathtaking views. The porters set up tents at the bottom of the tower as the rest of us begin to climb. I feel pretty winded by the time we reach the top. At 15,100 feet, this is the highest we've been so far. Seraphina and Leslie seem to be doing okay, although I hear Leslie complaining of a slight headache and a hint of nausea. I doubt anything will happen to Seraphina. She is what I would describe as chiseled—everything from her muscles to her facial features. I would bet that she's in the best shape of all of us, though Chris could give her a run for her money. He appears to be extraordinarily dedicated to his physical appearance too. Still, they say that mountain sickness can happen to anyone. So far, excluding Claire, everyone in our group has fared well.

From the top of Lava Tower, we can see the western part of Kibo in the distance, a place better known as the Western Breach. Clouds hover over this magnificent formation—the large outer rim that lava has carved into something that resembles a giant mummy-like figure lying flat on its back, with well-defined facial features and a slight belly bulge. Its "body" is covered in random, feathery paint strokes, which are actually spotty white glaciers. "As beautiful as it may appear," Simon explains, "the Western Breach is one of the most difficult and dangerous routes to summit Kilimanjaro." He tells the story of three hikers who were killed by a rock fall back in 2006, and a California entrepreneur who was killed in almost the exact same location by a falling boulder in 2018. Due to safety concerns, most tour companies, including Out Yonder, do not offer treks along this route, Simon says.

I am glad to have chosen Out Yonder and the Lemosho Route.

We stay a little longer at the top, admiring the kind of beauty that I've never before seen. The sound of "wow" and "whoa" floats freely through the thinnest air we've breathed yet. Chris captures what I'm sure are several amazing shots with his camera before we head down to the bottom of Lava Tower, where lunch awaits us.

▲ ▲ ▲

Today's lunch is like sitting way up in the sky at a table full of friends, sharing tea and sandwiches and Kachumbari (a relish-like African salad) while floating over a cloud floor below us. Simon tells more stories from past journeys to summit this great mountain and shows us more pictures of his daughter, Hediye. I am completely capti-vated by her. That hair. Those eyes. Her gorgeous smile. Everything about her is enamoring. I can see why his love for this precious lit-tle girl is vast.

Chris, who has been strangely quiet so far, suddenly asks Sera-phina and Leslie a bold question. "Do the two of you have any kids?"

Kids. My heart sinks, and my mind takes me back to what was supposed to be one of the happiest days of my life: the day the two pink lines appeared on the stark white background, and I was offi-

role, it sig...

We celebrated Baby Halleck that night, devouring Trish's ... Ranch casserole as we took bets on whether the baby was a boy or girl. We talked about potential names from both sides of our fami-lies. I may have even gotten emotional when Trish suggested naming a boy after my father—Thomas Richard—or a girl after my mother, Mary Patricia (Mary Pat, for short). I was glowing, they said.

A month later, another casserole arrived. This time, with grim faces. The baby was dead. There was no heartbeat on the ultrasound. There were no words to describe the devastation. Had Brody been addicted at this point, there's no telling what might have happened. I might have attempted to swallow several of those sorry pills myself.

I might not ever have kids now.

Chris's question lingers in the air around us for an uncomfortable moment. But Leslie snaps the tension with her sweet-as-pie voice.

"No kids yet," she says. "Our careers are so . . . demanding right now. I told Seraphina that I'd really like to work a few more years, then scale back to a couple of days a week so that I can be home with the baby most of the time."

We all smile, and Seraphina gazes at Leslie the way a husband or wife gazes at his or her new spouse on their wedding day. Thereafter, the conversation lags a bit, so Simon moves on to verbal new ground.

"I would like to ask you another question," he says to Seraphina as she swallows a bite of her sandwich. "May I call you 'Seri'? It is a lot to say, *Seraphina.*"

We all laugh. I like that Simon wants to use a nickname. It's a term of endearment that signifies the bond that is growing among us, like a shoelace sewing the laces of our group tighter together.

Seraphina nods. "Of course," she says, the usually pensive tone of her voice a little lighter now.

Dessert time approaches, and the porters deliver individually wrapped chocolate chip cookies to each of us. They aren't freshly baked, like my mother's famous ooey-gooeys—my nickname for my mother's delicious, piping hot chocolate chip dessert bars—but they are nevertheless tasty.

"Enjoy your calories, Seri and friends, for you will need them," Simon says. "*Safari lazima iendelee.*"

28

lower and ...

acclimatization exercise. We enter new territory, more aesthetically
pleasing than before. Steep, rocky terrain and an afternoon shower
make for slippery conditions that require trekking poles.

This stretch of our journey is particularly breathtaking. A crystal-
clear mountain stream runs downhill like moving glass. A waterfall
calls from the distance, sounding like a heavy downpour pounding
pavement on a hot summer day back home. I'd give anything to feel
the scorching summer sun in Arkansas right now, for the cold here is
merciless. Still, I brave the path ahead.

Interesting vegetation appears. Simon points out a giant ground-
sel, which towers over his head as he explains that these trees can
grow to be over ten feet tall. I marvel at its unique appearance—it
has a spiky brown tree trunk that reminds me of a giant pine cone
with what looks like a leafy-green head of cabbage sitting on top
of it. But instead of concave cabbage leaves, which cling tightly
together in a natural ball, these leaves point outward, like layered,

convex mini-swords. According to Simon, this plant is extremely resistant to the freezing temperatures up here, because the leaves can fold downward on top of the spiky trunk to provide insulation.

Chris snaps more pictures, and I can't blame him this time. These trees are crazy looking. Something like Florida palms gone wild in the middle of an apocalyptic wasteland.

The descent isn't altogether fulfilling. I'd rather be making progress toward the summit. But Simon reminds us that it is necessary. Having climbed to 15,000 feet or higher today, it is crucial that we find lower ground on which to sleep. Otherwise, we risk serious illness, the kind that took Claire and Casey off the mountain.

When we finally arrive at Barranco Camp, the porters have once again established our tiny tent village, and we are welcomed by dancing and singing of a caliber that I have not yet witnessed. Chants, handclaps, circles, smiles, and songs infect the village in the best kind of way. One porter grabs my arm and drags me into the circle. I am horrified. Another porter grabs Chris, and unlike me, he seems all in. The next thing I know, he is dancing with them, then dancing alone in the middle of our circle, clapping, moving his body to the sound of their voices. He's got natural rhythm. When he wags an index finger at me, inviting me to join him, I immediately shake my head. There is no way that I'm going out there. I haven't known fun in forever, only the responsibility of caring for Brody.

Chris's behavior seems slightly irresponsible, maybe even silly or immature. On the other hand, it also seems joyful. Purposeful. He is purposely spreading joy and inviting me into his circle of happiness. Isn't that why I came here? To find joy and purpose again?

Yes. Get out there, Marren.

Though I don't want to, I force myself into the middle of the circle, the music gaining momentum around me. I dance alongside Chris, who seems pleasantly surprised. Our hands are in the air now. Seri (as we all call her now) and Leslie join us. Their hands go up too. The sheer energy of our solidarity is more than apparent. In a unique way, we are quickly becoming family, right here on Mount Kilimanjaro.

A few minutes later, we disband for dinner, and Chris looks at me with eyes that are clearly hungry for something. Are they hungry for love? Sex? Companionship? Or are they hungry to get to know someone that he doesn't truly know, so that he can figure out whether he actually wants all of those other things? Whatever his reasons, I look back at him with the same hunger in my eyes. Except

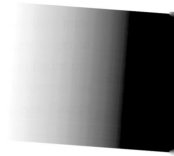

29

BUT FOR THE ENERGY of our trekking team and others, our campsite at Barranco would be desolate. Minus human presence, this cold and uninhabited valley might resemble a proverbial ghost town. Human connection has truly brought this place to life. Inside of Old Red, preparing for yet another evening meal, I take out my journal and begin to write. Once again, the speed of my thoughts far exceeds the speed of my writing. Words fly across the pages, full of the same kind of vigor that Chris brought to our dancing session earlier this afternoon.

Outside, something is snapping against the tent. I am hopeful that it is Chris. I unzip the front panel and pull back the nylon, but all I see is a loose flap. I am disappointed. The wind is particularly nasty tonight, picking up speed, pounding Old Red ferociously now. I return to my journal, seeking a temporary escape from its eerie howl.

Minutes later, Simon's voice calls from a distance, summoning us to dinner. Thankfully, the wind settles long enough for me to make it to the dining tent without a fight. Once there I run straight into Chris, whose eyes are greener than I've ever seen them.

"Ladies first," he says, smiling at me, and we enter the dining tent together.

▲ ▲ ▲

Tonight's dinner is a delectable arrangement of pork, potatoes, and eggplant. We gather around the table as Simon calls out our names.

"Marren, Chris, Seri, and Leslie!"

We all nod, a community response to Simon's roll call of sorts.

"I trust that you ﹍ ﹍ tonight's briefing, are there any questions?"

Leslie's syrupy voice fills the room. "I have a question," she says. There is a twinge of uncertainty in her voice that makes me think she's nervous. Something quickens in my own stomach, for anxiety is an emotion that I haven't yet associated with Leslie's personality.

"Yes?" Simon says.

"How hard is it to make it past the Barranco Wall?" Leslie asks.

I admire her courage to bring it up. I've read many blog pieces and online stories about the Barranco Wall. Some of them reassured me, others terrified me. Apparently, the Barranco Wall is the sole reason why some people wouldn't dare attempt to summit Kilimanjaro—it is arguably one of the most challenging parts of the entire expedition. I pay close attention to Simon's answer to the question.

In his typical positive mood, Simon reassures Leslie with stories about past trekkers. One, an older man who lost his footing and fell several feet down, gained only a few scratches and a confidence boost from his incident, eventually making it across on his second attempt. Another, a forty-something mother of three, simply did not think she could make it past something called the "leap of faith," which requires one to plant a foot in an unsteady crease and take hold of a guide's hand to be pulled to the next part of the wall.

"If these trekkers made it, the four of you can do it," Simon tells us. "The Barranco Wall won't be easy, but it won't be terrible, either. Think of it as a minor challenge. Nothing too severe. Nothing too mild."

Leslie appears to accept Simon's response. She seems back to herself, less worried now.

A steady flow of coffee, tea, and the allure of Simon's stories enhances our evening fellowship. The wind whips more fiercely as the outside temperature plummets, and we remain inside the dining tent for much longer than usual, trading stories from our pasts.

Seri goes first, telling us about her mother's struggle with alcohol addiction and chronic health problems. "I didn't want to leave her," she says, a subtle hint of pain resonating in her voice. "But Leslie convinced me that I needed this. Something for myself, for once. So here I am, ready to summit this mountain with the woman I love." Leslie smiles and takes Seri's hand, just before she begins to tell her own story.

Raised in New Orleans by a socialite mother and a father who was a partner in one of Louisiana's largest law firms, Leslie was born with a silver spoon in her mouth. She never really knew adversity, she tells us, until she met Seri in medical school and learned of Seri's mother's health issues. Leslie's glamorous compassion, together with Seri's fierce determination, seem to make them the perfect couple. Never mind that Leslie's parents no longer speak to her, and while Seri's mother is now sober, she is facing a life-altering battle with breast cancer.

Wow. I admire their authenticity. Something in the mountain air and the way that Seri and Leslie have so boldly shared their truths makes me want to share my own. So I do.

I tell them about my parents' accident. About Brody and our pity-based relationship. About the way he disintegrated into the hellish fires of hydrocodone's grip. About the girl into which I devolved. Eyes grow wide around me, and I suddenly feel like I have over-shared, until I turn to Chris, who is eyeing me again with that same look that made me feel as though he is hungry for something.

Suddenly, I understand. That nighttime green in his hazel eyes

money—quite a bit of it—in the seventies and eighties.

Chris pauses to take another sip of coffee.

"When my father died about ten years ago, my brother, Pete, took over the business—Courtland Oil. Pete was my best friend, my confidant. The only person in this world that understood where I came from, because we came from the same place. The same parents. The same upbringing. The same screwed-up family that no one else on earth could ever understand."

Chris takes a long, deep breath.

"Anyway, about a year ago, I got a call from my sister-in-law—Pete's wife. She was frantic, not making any sense. I tried to understand her words, but I couldn't. Everything she said was jumbled. The only thing I could make out was, 'Please, Chris! Please get over here now!' I got in my car and drove as fast as I could."

Chris paused briefly. I could hear a lump in his throat, clearly a sign of an unwillingness to continue.

"Not long after, I walked into my brother's house, where he lived with his wife and two-year-old twin girls, and I found him on the floor of his master bedroom, dead from a self-inflicted gunshot wound to the head."

Silence among us.

"I can't get it out of my mind," he says. "Him lying there, bloody and lifeless and cold in front of me. Me having to console his wife, Shaye. Having to look at those girls, Ava and Sydney. It's like a weight that's been chained to me forever."

More silence among us.

"I finally realized that I needed an escape. I started climbing mountains. It's the only way I know how to cope. To pick something so potentially difficult and demonstrate that I can handle it. Because honestly, I can't handle losing Pete. I don't know that I'll ever be able to handle it."

The wind pummels our dining tent now. Chris turns to me, as if I am the one with the right words to comfort him. But I have no idea what to say, so we all sit there, in complete silence.

30

scarce. Tonight,

imprisoned by the quiet darkness around me. I can't bear to toss and turn one more time, so I move to the kitchen and start researching mountains to climb on my laptop, because Brody told me to do it in my dream. I try to focus, but memories blindfold me and tie me up, trying to steal any hope I have for a future without him.

I think of the way that guilt held me hostage in my own home for all of these years. Of Brody's uncanny ability to make me feel responsible for his addiction. Of the fact that there wasn't a day that went by when he wouldn't throw guilt my way.

"It's always about *you*, Marren, You and your needy little emotions. You and your inability to get over the fact that your parents died. Just face it, Marren, people's parents *die*. You're not the only one. Get over it, already, and get me my medicine. It's time for you to start taking care of *me* now." And on and on and on.

The guilt trip never stopped. Whenever I suggested that he get some help, as I often did, he'd always punt things right back on me.

"*Me* get some help? *You're* the one that needs help, Marren. You don't even know how to support your own husband. You never supported me in my baseball career. Hell, you remember the time you missed the semi-final state championship game? Our senior year?"

I was taken aback. This was not the man I married.

"Brody, I was attending an event to honor my father at the Rotary Club. He'd just died, for Pete's sake! Oh my God! Who are you? I was there for every single game except that one. I can't believe—"

"Oh, just shut up. You know you never supported me. You were so jealous of me you could spit. So jealous of my family. The one you were never going to have after the accident. Admit it."

The conversation is difficult to remember. We exchanged these words on a random Saturday afternoon, when Brody was running short on pills. When the handful of doctors in Clear Springs—unlike the ocean of them in Little Rock—had picked up on Brody's visits.

He'd never hit me before. But that would soon change.

He begged me to make an appointment with my own doctor, to fake a back injury and complain of unbearable pain so that I could secure a gleaming new supply of hydrocodone—not for myself but for him. It was a plausible plan, a way to buy some valuable time before the next refill from his doctor.

As appalled as I was at his suggestion, I initially agreed to it, for I knew that anything less might send him into a frenzy. One day's delay of his wrath was a small victory, I told myself. Except it wasn't.

When he awoke that next day, he discovered that I hadn't made the appointment and I didn't have the pills. He had very few left, and he immediately began to panic. His demeanor became increasingly more disturbing, with hints of violence that made me cringe. Mania ensued. He left a hole in the wall that was the size of his fist. I tried my best to avoid him, but he wouldn't let it go. The end result was the confrontation in the master bathroom, just after I'd gotten out of the shower and was drying my hair.

"You will get those pills for me," he said. "Won't you?" The desperation in his voice was evident. For a moment, I felt the tiniest bit of pity for him.

"Brody, I can't. It's not right. I won't lie for you."

He immediately became belligerent, and the tone of his voice grew frightening.

"Yes, you will. You will do it today. You will call Dr. Shepherd and tell him about your pain."

"Brody, I can't—"

_____ _____ fell from my hands, still humming as he grabbed

Only then did I agree.

"Yes," I said. "Yes, I will call Dr. Shepherd. I will tell him about the pain. I'll get the pills. Please, please. Don't hurt me again."

31

MORNING SUN POURS into my freezing tent, and my feet wrestle with two Nalgene water bottles that are buried at the base of my sleeping bag. It's a trick I read about before the trip—fill two Nalgene bottles with boiling water and place them at the base of your sleeping bag to keep your feet warm on the mountain. Needless to say, the warm bottles have turned cold now, but they sure felt good last night. I am proud of myself for learning how to boil my own water on a mountain. The porters offered to do it for me, but I refused. I've watched a million YouTube videos on how to do this. And I did it. It's one small step toward learning how to survive on my own.

Now, I am awake but still very tired. The frigid temperatures have robbed me of sleep, but golden rays are peering their way in, reminding me of new day ahead. For some reason, my stomach is reeling with regret. I turn over and pull the sleeping bag tighter around me, hoping this feeling will go away. Instead, it intensifies. Something is wrong, but I don't know what.

I lie in my sleeping bag, shivering, loathing the idea that I will soon have to emerge and brave the biting cold. No matter how many layers of high-end Spyder or Arc'teryx outerwear that I put on, I will still be cold on this mountain. No matter how many cups of coffee I consume, I will still lack genuine clarity in life. And no matter how many times I talk about Brody, I will still be ashamed.

I told everyone about Brody.

It hits me like lightning from nowhere, a flashback to our post-dinner sharing session. Brody is here forever now, on this mountain with me. I can no longer escape him—because everyone knows my truth. I think of Seri's struggles with her mother, along with Chris's

̶ ̶ ̶ ̶ ̶brother—his very best friend in the

me, so I wiggle—
another day of this journey.

When I finally arrive at the breakfast tent, Chris sits alone with his coffee drink. He looks so masculine, so adventurous under his green and brown layers of clothing, which remind me of the setting around us. I'm suddenly happy that Seri and Leslie aren't here yet. I can't wait to sit down next to him, a chance for some more time alone together. We share a new kind of trauma bond.

Strangely, he doesn't acknowledge my arrival. That feeling in my stomach returns. This new silence between us is thick and apparent, confusing. Why isn't he saying anything to me?

"Good morning," I say.

He nods silently.

I am deflated. My stomach churns. Is something wrong?

One of the porters brings me a coffee and asks me if I'd like some eggs and porridge. I say yes, and Chris doesn't say anything. This is definitely not how I want to begin today, a day when we are supposed to tackle the Barranco Wall—an eight-hundred-foot journey up steep and difficult terrain that is sure to send me into full panic mode.

The porter returns with my breakfast, and I swirl the spoon around in my lumpy porridge, suddenly hopeful that Seri and Leslie will show up soon. Chris is staring at his copy of *Lonesome Dove*, sipping his coffee, still intriguingly quiet.

Finally, I can't take any more.

"What's wrong with you?" I ask.

He turns his gaze to me, the morning blue in his eyes piercing into mine. This look is nothing like the one he's given me before. It is not an endearing look. It is a painful one.

"Come on, Marren," he says. "You know what's wrong. Let's not play games. Not here. Not now."

I honestly have no idea what he means.

"What are you talking about?" I say.

He slams his coffee cup on the table, obviously serious. "You mean to tell me that you don't remember last night? Did you sneak some vodka up here or something?"

What?

Of course I remember last night. Our time around the dinner table. The moment I shared my secret about Brody. Seri's discussion about her mother. Chris's heartbreaking story of finding his brother dead on the floor. Everything is one-hundred-percent clear in my mind.

"Yes," I say. "Of course I remember. I remember *everything*."

"Then you know what I'm talking about."

"We all told our secrets," I say. "We all shared our stories. I thought that was a good thing."

A look of disbelief forms in his eyes.

"I'm talking about *after* that," he says, shaking his head.

After that? Now *after that*, I don't remember.

126

"Oh, don't pretend like it didn't happen, Marren," he says, in a most patronizing tone. "We were in your tent, after our dinner-time tell-all, and I told you more than I've ever told anyone about what happened to Pete. I felt like I could tell you anything. I felt so strongly about the connection between us that I kissed you. And then . . . you called me Brody."

I did? Oh, no. I really *don't* remember.

"Let's get one thing straight, okay? I'm not *Brody*. And I can't possibly get involved with someone who thinks that I am. So I _____ Because I really like you,

You and me. He a

Suddenly, Seri and Leslie appear, bundled in brightly colored Patagonia gear.

"Good morning, all!" Seri announces, her beautiful white smile launching watts of energy throughout the tent.

Chris immediately changes his tone, and it's as if nothing bad has ever transpired between us. Seri and Leslie sit down at the table, and day five of our journey begins. Once again, our unfinished conversation will have to wait. I'll have to scale the Barranco Wall in spite of his anger. This is going to be the hardest day yet.

32

THE BARRANCO WALL is a steep, rocky, volcanic cliff-like formation, the result of gradual collapses and landslides after Kilimanjaro went dormant several hundreds of thousands of years ago, Simon explains. Known as the "breakfast wall" (because you have to tackle it first thing as you begin the day), it is a place where many of the routes to the summit of Kilimanjaro—the Lemosho, the Machame, the Umbwe, and the Shira—all meet. There is much traffic here, and Simon recommends that we let others go before us so as to avoid crowded conditions. He reminds us of two important things before we begin our ascent up the wall: first, the value of pressure breathing, which is taking in a slow, deep breath followed by quickly blowing it out, and second, remembering to "kiss the wall" along one of the more daunting parts of Barranco, where the terrain becomes so narrow that it is necessary to keep your face and hands very close to the rock wall so as not to look down.

Once again, I think of everything I've read about this wall, especially the questions about whether amateurs could make it past this technical part of the climb. Almost everything I read said yes, that it really didn't require advanced technical skills—just concentration and the ability to "scramble" at times up along its narrow, back-and-forth path. While these words reassured me then, I'm not so sure now. The sight of this vast wall is daunting. My brain reminds me that one false move—one tiny moment of sheer panic—could send me tumbling five hundred feet. The thought of this brings a prickle of sweat to my hands and brow.

I can do this. I can do this.

As we come to the base of the wall, we wait out the traffic jam ney. So I remain silent too.

At first, there is a lot of waiting. The trail is narrow enough to accommodate only a single-file line in most places. This gives me more time to worry.

We press on to steeper territory, and the fact that Chris is not speaking to me makes the trail even more taxing. Finally, we come to the place where we must "kiss the wall." This is the part I've been dreading for the entire trip. It's not as narrow as I envisioned, but still, it's *narrow*. At this point, I'm playing a mind game: *Barranco Wall vs. Marren Halleck*. Whoever possesses the most equanimity to persevere will come away with a victory.

Simon makes it across. Chris makes it across. And then suddenly, it's my turn.

I am certain that I can't do it. My hands tremble. Sweat pools on my forehead. My heart feels like a ticking time bomb. I look back at the line of people who are waiting on me to do this. They are staring at me. More pressure builds. I want to cry, but that won't help.

"*Pole, pole,* Marren. You can do this!" says Simon. In Swahili, "pole" means "slowly." I know this from my pre-trip research—watching hundreds of YouTube videos on climbing Kilimanjaro. I heed Simon's advice. If I rush now, the outcome will surely be grim.

"*Pole, pole!*" Simon says again. His voice coaxes me to inch forward, practically gluing myself to the wall, promising myself that I will not look down.

I will not panic. I will not panic. I will just move forward, inch by inch, kissing the wall, holding it tight like an alpine lover.

"You've got this," Leslie says from behind me. That sweet voice again, almost like sugar. If I could bottle up that voice and sell it, I'd make a mint off the sweet-toothed customers. The thought of Leslie's voice in a bottle distracts me in a good way, shifting my focus from fear to Leslie and her encouragement.

I move at a snail's pace, finding a slow rhythm that seems to be working. I keep my eyes on the prize of wider trail ahead, where Simon and Chris are waiting for me. *Hold on to me, lover,* I say to the mountain, and I feel it squeeze me back.

I can do this.

My confidence returns. The mountain is holding on to me, protecting me.

"*Pole, pole,* Marren. *Pole, pole!*" Simon cheers.

I am almost there.

Suddenly, my foot slips. Terror ensues. I look down to see that my foot is hanging on to the edge by an inch, maybe two. *You cannot do it! You cannot do this!* Voices scream in my head. *You are going to die!*

A full panic attack is coming on. I can feel it. I used to think that panic attacks only happened to crazy people. And then I witnessed them personally, throughout Brody's battle with hydrocodone.

A few years back, before I knew that Brody had a full-blown addiction, we'd been driving to Little Rock to visit one of his old teammates, when suddenly, he swerved over the center line.

"Oh my God! Brody, what's wrong?"

Chaos followed. He was sweating, claiming to be dizzy, scream-ing that he couldn't see, that everything was going black. I grabbed the steering wheel, begging him to take his foot off the gas pedal, praying that I could control the car sufficiently from the passenger seat to steer us over to the shoulder.

"What happened?" I asked him when we were finally safe, hav-ing come to a stop.

"I don't know. I just got dizzy. I couldn't see. I felt like I was going

down   my anxiety is

Chris steps into my line of sig

me. "Remember what we talked about, Marren. You're *fine*. Just a little foot slip. Gently move it back to where it was, and slowly con-tinue on. Don't think about what you are doing. Think about the piña colada on the beach that I told you to think of when you were so cold yesterday."

His words enter my heart, and it warms again, just like it did before.

I move my foot back to a more solid position, and I inch along, kissing the wall, thinking about that piña colada. It's as if a calming buzz has come over me from an imaginary cocktail.

Before I know it, I've made it across the kissing wall, and every-one erupts in applause, even Chris. He gives me a high five, and suddenly, peace forms between us. I wish I had that piña colada now, sitting somewhere on a beach with Chris.

33

AT THE TOP of the Barranco Wall, the views are incredible. A cluster of clouds sails along in the blue sky over the valley below us. Gorgeous views of Kibo's peak and Mount Meru seep through them in the distance.

The terrain is now flat and easy to navigate. Simon and Chris walk up ahead of me in the distance as we begin our descent into the Karanga Valley. Seri and Leslie stroll along behind us, arm in arm. It's an absolutely gorgeous day, with miles of blue sky and plentiful sunshine to accentuate the greenish-gray-brown territory ahead.

Though I am walking alone, I am genuinely happy. *This is what happiness must feel like—the simple, easy, basic joy of being content with my surroundings.* I am not rich or famous. I am not married to a handsome, rich husband with smart, athletic kids who are bound for Harvard and major league baseball contracts. I am simply Marren, walking through uncomplicated terrain on the way to the Karanga Camp, breathing in life around me, thankful for the opportunity to be here now. I am *happy*.

Simon announces that we're stopping briefly to rest and hydrate. I pull out my water bottle and take a long, grateful drink, when Chris comes up to me.

"You did great today," he says.

I can't help but smile.

He returns the smile. The situation is still awkward. So I dive into the discomfort between us.

"I honestly don't know why I said that last night," I say. "I mean, ˙ ˙saving it. The only thing I remember after And nothing

"Am I supp˙

a sudden? You sure you didn't take some˙˙˙ ˙ Tell me the truth, Marren."

I feel cornered, like some kind of defendant on trial in court.

"You have to believe me. I don't have any drugs or alcohol. After what I went through with Brody, I'm very careful about that stuff." *Yeah, right. I can definitely overdo it on the wine sometimes.* But I don't have any with me on this mountain.

Chris's eyes meet mine, and in that moment, I sense that I am beginning to convince him.

"Besides," I say, "I couldn't bring that stuff up here anyway. It would take up too much space in my duffel. I'd exceed the weight limit."

Chris laughs. I laugh. Our moment of shared laughter connects us in a strange new way. Still, I seek vindication, some sort of explanation for the fact that I cannot remember a single thing that happened last night. Something as important as an intimate moment between Chris and me, when I would dare to call him Brody.

And then it comes to me. I know what it could be.

When researching things that could go wrong on a Kilimanjaro climb (which I often did), I came across an article about a woman who was recovering from cancer and decided to take on the challenge of summiting Mount Kilimanjaro. During her expedition, she suffered repeated bouts of short-term memory loss and hallucination—likely due to oxygen deprivation from the high altitude.

"That has to be it. There's no other explanation," I say.

"What are you talking about?" Chris says.

"I must have been *hallucinating*, thinking you were Brody. It's this altitude thing—I can't remember what they call it." I search my mind for the term that the article used. "High-altitude hypoxic amnesia!" I say excitedly. "That's what they call it."

Chris narrows his eyes as he takes a sip from his water bottle, appearing to doubt me. Simon announces that we're leaving in five minutes.

"Time to go, Mare."

Mare? He's never called me by a nickname. *A step in the right direction, for sure.*

He walks off, playfully slaps Simon on the back, and looks back at me as he nods his head in the direction of the trail ahead, summoning me to join him.

I can see the skyline of our campsite way off in the distance, and it looks like we are close enough to reach it very soon. I remind myself that as near as it seems, we are still hours away. I think of childhood trips to the Florida panhandle, walking hand-in-hand along the beach with my father next to emerald-green water, unable to take my eyes off the tall buildings on the horizon. We'd walk and walk, never seeming to get much closer to them. They appeared so reachable, but in reality they were a half day's walk from us. Back then, I could just tell my daddy that I was tired and turn around. Here, that's not an option.

Safari lazima iendelee. The journey must continue.

34

the rocky zigzags of the ~~

takes a toll on my legs, causing strain on muscles I never even knew
I had. My knees buckle often, the momentum testing various parts
of my anatomy—mostly my quads.

Finally, we reach a point where we must start uphill again, and
our desire to go on is running on empty. Simon brings new energy,
breaking out into his own special version of "Hakuna Matata"
(which means "no worries" in Swahili). Everyone except Chris
begins to belt out the lyrics like little children. I am disappointed
that he is not participating. I want to see the post-dinner-celebration
Chris, the one who isn't afraid to let it all hang out, so I hold a trekking pole up to my face like it's a microphone, and then I share it
with Seri and Leslie while Chris laughs at us. At least he is laughing.
Once again, Simon has renewed our team spirit.

Now, heading uphill to the Karanga Camp, our final destination
for the day, we are problem free, at least in song.

▲ ▲ ▲

At Karanga Camp, our group poses for a picture in front of Kilimanjaro's spectacular, snow-capped summit, perfectly positioned in the background behind us. The image rests vividly in my phone; I can't stop staring at it. It is my favorite one from the trip thus far. So inspiring and majestic, full of people I'm growing to love.

Dinner is a delicious combination of pork chops, ugali (corn cake), and green beans. The mood is much lighter than last night. There is much laughter around the dinner table as Simon shares funny stories about his daughter. The way she once said a Swahili curse word in front of strangers and how he was mortified. The way she once ran off through a village screaming wildly, scared to death of a plate of sizzling meat. Every story is enhanced by the adoring tone in his voice. I can tell that Simon is a good man, a funny man, a smart man.

An *authentic* man.

I'm starting to believe that some of the best and happiest people on planet earth lead the most authentic of lives, like Simon's. He is obviously true to himself.

Dessert is authentic too. It is Simon's favorite—some sort of light, spongy shortcake, topped with strawberries in a sugary syrup. Chris is next to me again. Since our talk in the Karanga Valley, he has been more attentive. I can't say I don't enjoy it.

The porters begin their nightly routine of chants and songs around the campfire, and Chris opts to join them again. He nods in their direction, coercing me to join him, but I shake my head and return to my tent. This time I stand my ground. I feel a bit like a bore, but I'd rather be alone with Old Red tonight. I just want to journal or sink into my sleeping bag with a good book.

Ten minutes later, I'm snuggled in tight. Nalgene bottles are toasting my feet. I pick up "The Snows of Kilimanjaro" again, but then I remember that I brought a couple of other paperbacks with me, some recommendations from trusted Facebook reading groups.

I read a lot of books during Brody's worst days. My favorites were the ones who could take me to bold new places, ones where I could escape my desperate reality. Goodness knows I needed to escape from my world into someone else's back then. Now, I have escaped to this mountain.

I dig out *Wild* by Cheryl Strayed, a highly recommended story of escape. It will be perfect tonight.

patterns.

He climbs in, a bit sunburned and grimy from the day's events. I can tell that he is still high on the energy from dancing and chanting and singing with the porters. He settles into a corner opposite from me.

"I'm sorry I was such a jerk to you," he says.

I'm shocked by his candid words.

"It's okay," I say. "I'm sorry that things happened the way they did. And that I can't even remember it!"

He smiles. I am so attracted to him at this point that I feel myself getting awkward, nervous. And when I get nervous, I tend to be too forward.

"So, tell me, what really happened last night? What did I say? What did you say?"

His eyes widen; apparently he's impressed with my bold questions.

"Well," he says. "After I shared my story, you invited me to your tent to talk about it, almost like some sort of therapist."

I feel myself turning red. How could I possibly not remember something like that?

"And I accepted. We talked for almost two hours. About Pete. I've never met anyone that made me feel like I wanted to tell them about Pete. It was like you lifted a load off my back. I knew when I first looked at you that I could trust you. That you were the right person to tell."

His words are bringing me new life, like water to a wilted flower.

"Things just felt so good, so right. I had to do it. So I kissed you. And then, like I told you before, you called me *Brody*."

I feel myself begin to wilt.

"It hurt, Marren."

I shake my head. Tears are welling in my eyes. I have no idea what to say.

"Anyway, I started thinking about it this morning. About your pain. Everything that you've had to deal with. We haven't really talked about Brody. You haven't really told me everything about your struggle. And I haven't really told you everything about mine. When I saw you scared on that wall today, I realized how much I care about you. There's just something about you that makes me want to know you more. I'm sorry. And I'm here to ask if we can start over again."

A tear streams down my left cheek. I cannot contain it. And I realize now that I cannot contain my feelings for Chris either. I reach out to hug him, and he hugs me back. But just when I think he's going to try and kiss me again, he stops.

"*Pole, pole,*" he says.

That's how we're going to take things now, as we head up this mountain together. Slowly, slowly.

35

Drip-drop. Another morning

sure I can't face it. I pull the covers over my head again, groggy with grief. I want to get up and go for a run, but I'm far too tired. There is not one ounce of me that wants to escape from the refuge of these covers, not one part of my soul that's ready to face what's ahead.

My husband is dead.

I hear my phone ping, and I conjure the energy to reach for it. The words on the screen are blurry, distorted by the morning fog that still resides inside my head. When the message finally comes into focus, I see that it is a text from Molly Hale—my lifelong best friend who used to be like a sister. Since Brody's addiction, however, I've pushed her away.

How are you, Marren? I hope you are okay. The funeral was beautiful. I miss you. If you ever want to talk, I'm here.

Drip, drop, drip. My insides tingle with nostalgia—Molly and I haven't really talked in years now. I miss our talks. The kind where we'd sit on Molly's parents' porch, wine coolers in hand, just a couple of teenage girls dreaming about their futures.

We'd talk for hours about where our lives were headed. Whether Brody would ask me to marry him. What our kids would look like. Whether Molly would end up with Brett, her on-again, off-again boyfriend. How much I missed my mom and dad. How much she did too. I could really use one of those talks right now.

I miss having a best friend, someone who knows almost everything about me and still loves me anyway. Someone who's been there for me through thick and thin. Someone who knows my deepest, darkest secrets. Someone like Molly. She knows me. Except she doesn't. She doesn't know about the pills. And I'm not sure I can tell her.

Molly and I met when we were six years old, fellow first-grade brunettes, both of us obsessed with Mariah Carey. Our moms became fast friends and would often sit around with their afternoon wine, watching Molly and me dress up and lip sync the words to "Fantasy" and "Hero." Molly and I used to share everything, and I do mean everything. Bows. Outfits. CDs. Crushes on boys. Hours of tears after the accident. A six pack of beer on our high school graduation night.

I saw Molly from a distance at Brody's funeral. Though we never spoke directly, I did notice that her once-black hair was now a lighter chestnut brown. She stood across the room from me—this sweet girl who'd been my best friend for almost my entire life. She was the first one I'd told when Brody asked me out. The first to know about our very first kiss and the first time Brody made love to me at his parents' house when they were away. The first to wish me luck on a calculus test, and the only person in the world that knew about my secret crush on Leonardo DiCaprio (I didn't want to hurt Brody's feelings). She was also the maid of honor at my wedding.

Now, she is practically a stranger.

Over time, our friendship had bent, but certainly never broken—until the pills arrived. After that, I transformed into a vault, locking my reality away inside for absolutely no one to see. I didn't want to admit that my life was falling apart, that my marriage was beyond repair. I was supposed to be the girl with the fairy-tale life. The princess who married her handsome, kind, athletic prince and lived happily ever after. But I couldn't tell her the truth, so our friendship had slowly unraveled. I avoided Molly's calls and texts, and we were never really the same again.

dering if it could ever

ship with Molly. And my entire life,

I shut off my phone and fall back asleep, and I don't wake up until the early afternoon.

36

THE SUN RISES majestically on the east side of Kilimanjaro, aiming its red-orange glow straight into my eyes, reminding me that today is a new day. It is July 10—the day that would have been my seventh wedding anniversary with Brody.

Lucky number seven. Or maybe the seven-year itch.

For better or worse, Brody and I will never reach these marital milestones.

It is the first anniversary that I've spent without him. Part of me hoped that being in Africa—far away, on a mountain with the focus being on climbing it—would mitigate the pain. In a strange way, it has, but on the other hand, there is a constant, searing anguish inside of me, a knife stuck in my side that I cannot remove. I must learn to live with it somehow. I must accept the fact that I will never celebrate another wedding anniversary on July 10.

As I force myself from my sleeping bag, I'm reminded of what Ella Nicole Spencer—the divorced protagonist from one of my favorite books, *We're All Hiding Something*, once told herself about her anniversary date after the divorce: "Someday, this day will feel like any other, just another ordinary day, with only the slightest twinge that something's not right."

That day is not today. The twinge is more like a tidal wave.

I drag myself to breakfast. My appetite seems to know what day it is today too. It mourns with me. The sausage and eggs and toast just don't look good to me right now. I sip on some coffee quietly as Simon prepares for the day's trek from Karanga to Barafu. Chris asks me if I'm okay. I smile and answer him in the cheeriest voice I can muster.

have spoken many times

back home in Arkansas,

feast on some toddler's lost Cheeto—except its neck is solid white.

I am fascinated by the way the bird lands on Simon's arm and just sits there. I look at Chris, who is standing next to Simon, and he smiles at me, seemingly impressed too.

"This is Karanga," Simon says. "A white-necked raven that visits the camp so often that we've named him after it. White-necked ravens are very smart. Some say as smart as a seven-year-old human."

Seven. That word again.

I will not cry.

I focus on Simon and the bird, hoping to fend off this pesky grief. The bird is as smart as a human? How can a bird be as smart as a human?

"Just watch, if you will," Simon says. Karanga rests gently on Simon's arm, and Simon looks down at him. "Karanga, say 'hello.'"

The bird looks up, his charcoal beak pointed straight at Simon, and repeats Simon's words.

"Say hello," the bird says.

Our group erupts in laughter.

"Karanga, say 'hi,'" Simon commands.

The bird looks around at all of us, then turns back to Simon. "Hi."

Simon smiles.

"Hi, hi, hi," the bird cackles. "Helllloooo!"

I laugh so hard that tears follow. Happy ones.

Simon speaks again.

"Karanga, say 'bye.'"

The bird obeys. "Bye. *Bye, bye, bye.*" And then he flies away, off into the distance.

As fast as he is here, showing off his talents, he is gone, and we are left to the challenge of the day ahead. This is another reminder of Brody. He and his talent have also gone, leaving me to the challenge of life alone. I glance up at the summit of Kilimanjaro in the distance, and suddenly it looks scarier than ever, a monstrous creature made of sharp, soaring, jagged body parts. Doubt lurks within me—I'm not sure that I can do it.

Chris walks up and puts a hand on my shoulder. "You ready?"

The energy of his touch tells me that I can.

"Yes," I say. We head back to our tents to pack up.

Happy anniversary, Brody. I will conquer this mountain.

▲ ▲ ▲

The journey from Karanga to Barafu takes us uphill into the arid mountain desert again, requiring us to navigate steep, rocky areas that resemble large, deep craters on the moon. Today, we will acclimatize to our highest level yet—just a bit higher than the top of

Lava Tower. I am perpetually amazed by the porters carrying heavy loads and water on the tops of their heads around us. It is almost impossible for me to carry my own daypack, which is far lighter, along this challenging terrain.

As Chris walks beside me, there is a comforting silence between us, much different than the silence of yesterday, when he was angry and I was oblivious. Gone are the beautiful flora and fauna and wildlife of the biomes below. I try not to allow this barren and desolate area to bring my spirits down. I've been down for years now, and I've come to this place to go up—physically and emotionally.

arctic abyss—much like the later years of my marriage to Brody.

"When I first met him, he was wonderful," I say, feeling slightly short of breath. I can tell the air is thinning. My limbs are heavier and my breathing more labored from the stress of continuing uphill.

"Oh?"

"He was a baseball player. A really good one." I take a necessary breath as we climb higher. "He played in college. And then in the minor leagues in Arkansas."

"How proud you must have been," he says. "Go on."

The changing elevation is requiring me to speak slowly, carefully, using every ounce of oxygen in the most efficient manner possible.

"He always treated me like a queen. He was a real gentleman. Everyone loved him."

I pause, not for lack of breath, but for the will to verbally continue.

Chris looks at me affectionately, apparently unfazed by the increasing altitude or emotion.

"And?"

"And then he got hurt. A rotator cuff injury. They put him on opioids, and the rest . . . well, I guess it's history. The catastrophic kind, like wartime or the Great Depression. Things were never the same."

Chris stops climbing and comes nearer to me. He draws me into his arms, holding my body against his. The stale, sweaty aroma of his clothing smells good to me. He holds on for a few seconds, and I wonder when he'll finally let go. I don't want him to. In the cocoon of his grasp, I am safe. I haven't felt so secure in a very long time.

I pull in tighter to his chest. He rubs the back of my head gently with his fingers. When he finally does let go, I sense a special warmth in his comforting gaze.

Please kiss me. Please.

Thankfully, we've fallen behind the rest of the group, so no one can see us. It would be the perfect time for a kiss.

Please.

Tears linger in the back of my eyes, along with the need to tell him.

"Today is our anniversary," I say. "We would have been married for seven years."

The look on his face changes a bit, and I feel foolish when I realize that now is not an appropriate time for a kiss, and that the thought is probably furthest from his mind. I bury my head into his shoulder, trying to hide away, but then he pulls my face into his hands.

"I'm so sorry, Mare. But I promise you that someday, it's all gonna be okay."

I close my eyes.

"Will it?" I ask.

He nods, then wraps me up into his arms. I sob into his chest. "Yes."

I don't believe him. But his arms feel so good around me that I want to. I really, really want to.

37

camp before summiting. Simon

official sign-in—a kind of formal registration where each group is
asked to record the names of all group members and their job titles,
the date, the name of the camp, and the name of our guide and out-
fitter. When we're done, Chris looks at me proudly.

"Well," he says. "Now it's official. Tomorrow's the big day. We
can do this, Marren."

We. I love the sound of that.

The wind picks up as we return to our crew, who is struggling to
set up the cook tent and dining tent. Chris and Seri and Leslie and
I put on our balaclavas and jump in to help. We fight wind speeds
of what Simon estimates to be above forty miles per hour, and at
times, it appears that the tents may actually go flying. Finally, with
a group effort, we are able to stabilize the stakes enough that the
tents are able to withstand the intense blasts of air. We eat dinner
early in these extremely unpleasant conditions, the wind whipping

so violently against the dining tent that I cannot concentrate on the food on my plate.

Simon attempts to talk over the whacking sound of the wind, giving us a detailed briefing on how to prepare for the summit.

"All right, Out Yonder crew," he begins. "Tonight, you will go to bed early, and I will wake you at 11:00 p.m. You will not like this."

We all laugh. Our laughter is muffled by the fierce roar of the wind outside.

"You will need to dress warmly," Simon tells us. "With layers of long underwear, ski pants, and a thick jacket. Take your headlamps for light and a balaclava for wind protection. We will leave here at midnight, after breakfast, and we will begin slowly walking up the mountain, through a sometimes harsh, icy-cold trail, until we reach Stella Point at 5,750 meters. From there, we will go another 145 meters to Uhuru Peak, the summit of Kilimanjaro, or the 'roof of Africa,' as we call it, at 5,895 meters."

The wind is extremely cruel now, and a cloud of concern falls over Simon's face as he turns to look at the side of the tent, which has come undone.

"All right, then, I'd like for each of you to get back to your tents to shelter in place for now, until these strong winds pass. Do not come outside—it isn't safe."

I wonder if I should worry, because if it isn't safe to be standing outside, how can it possibly be safe to attempt to summit the mountain? Chris must be picking up on my fear, because he asks if he can come back to my tent with me. Given his earlier message, that he wants to take things slowly, I'm curious about this request.

He follows me back to Old Red, each of us battling the flagellation of our clothing as we shield our eyes with our arms, struggling to remain upright. This glacial mountain air, beating against us now at what Simon said was somewhere around fifty miles per hour, is like taking the coldest, most brutal lashing in the world. I exhale deeply when I finally get to Old Red, practically falling inside.

Chris dives in after me, and we are suddenly on our backs together, sheltered from the harsh wind. I roll over to see him smiling, almost laughing, and I boldly wriggle over next to him, arranging his arm around my shoulder as I lie against his warm body. He doesn't protest. Instead, we just lie there together, looking up at the roof of the tent, listening to the eerie sound of wind trying to tear it away.

I feel his hand in my hair, stroking it softly. This sends a warm ͏ ͏ ͏ ͏ ͏ that I am being cared for. It's as

his arms, ͏ ͏ ͏ ͏ ͏

I'm sitting upright, detached from him now, and there doesn't seem to be a good way to return to the emotional embrace that we were just sharing. So I offer up some nervous conversation.

"You asked me what Brody was like," I say. "Now, it's my turn. You told me that we talked about Pete the other night in my tent. The night I still can't remember. I'd love a second chance. So tell me, what did you say?"

It isn't easy for me to ask Chris this, but I genuinely want to know more. I wonder if this will upset him. It doesn't, as he jumps right in. "Well," he begins. "Are you sure you'll remember it this time?"

I smile and nod. Clarity is ever-present now. Chris pulls me into him again, and I relax. We settle back into our snuggling position—his hand cradles my shoulder, and he begins to stroke my hair again.

"Pete was my hero," Chris says, his voice full of admiration. "The big brother that everyone wants. He was smart like my father, but less of an asshole. He was more like my mother, before she started drinking to cope with my father's crap."

I can feel his grip on my shoulder tighten as another frightening crackle hits the tent, an unexpected, whip-like sound that clearly startles us both. This time, I don't flinch.

"Everyone loved Pete. For everything from his diplomacy to his fascinating blue eyes to his fierce drive to succeed. The way he always made a point to treat people fairly, kindly. Even his striking cleft chin drew people to him. I think a lot of folks couldn't wait for my father to die so that Pete could take over Courtland Oil."

Wow. I want to meet him based on this short description alone.

"The day I found him forever changed me. No one can possibly understand the trauma of seeing someone you love so much lying in a pool of blood on the floor. And the thought of never being able to speak to him again, to ask his opinion on something or talk shit about someone that I can't stand in a way that only he can understand, to never hear his voice or see him again . . . It's just, well . . . I can't take it sometimes. And the only thing I know how to do is to avoid, to try and prove to myself that I'm strong enough to survive, even when he didn't. I constantly search my head for answers, for things I could have done to prevent him from taking that gun and ending his life. For words I could have said to make him see that he couldn't possibly leave Shaye and Ava and Sydney behind."

The wind hits the tent so hard that I quiver, burrowing deeper into Chris for protection. He holds me tighter, and I'm not sure what to say to ease his pain. And then I am.

"There's nothing you could have done, Chris," I tell him, relaxing my weight into him. "Sometimes, things happen that we can't ever have foreseen. Trust me, I know."

He pulls me closer.

"It must have been awful to lose Brody," he says.

"It was," I say. "Just like you said . . . it changes you forever."

I think of Brody's smile and the way it could once transform me. I see my parents, sitting at the dinner table, inviting me to share the best and worst parts of my day. I don't know which loss was worse. Should I tell Chris more about the accident? Maybe. But not now. One tragedy at a time.

"Oh, Mare. Finally, someone who understands."

There it is again, his referral to me as "Mare." Something about the way he says it just makes everything a little easier.

"Can I ask you a big favor?" he says.

... I'll say next.

"I need you to promise ... here tonight."

I laugh, and so does he.

"I solemnly swear," I say.

And then we fall asleep together, to the tune of the wind ripping its way through the Barafu Camp outside, readying ourselves for the ultimate part of this journey: the summit to Uhuru.

38

AFTER IGNORING MOLLY'S MESSAGE, I try to go back to sleep, but I can't get Brody's funeral out of my head. I turn over and reach for my phone, which is flooded with texts and missed calls from George and Trish, who so obviously pity me. This brings no comfort, for I recall what pity has done in my life. It made Brody stay with me after the accident, and it made me stay with Brody through his addiction.

I don't want pity anymore. I want out.

Another day comes and goes. The sun falls from the sky, a red-orange bandit, showing up to steal my joy and then run away, leaving only darkness behind. I am lost in this darkness now, a disoriented traveler searching for the way ahead. But for my internet searches, I have no course in life.

I decide to pull up the account with the inheritance money from my parents. I haven't looked at it in ages, because I can't stand the pang in my stomach that I get every single time I log in. But now that Brody is gone, I need to start working through my financial situation—to assess what I have and what I need to do from here—because, frankly, since Brody got hurt and had to give up his career as a professional baseball player, we haven't had much income. So I go to the Webster Financial site and type in my username and password. I click on "Account Overview," and when I do, my mouth drops open.

The balance is at a mere $3,489.

Oh, my god. Where did it go? My parents left me well over $250,000 in life insurance and other assets. We used a little of it for housing and other costs, but a little under half of the original amount should still be here. *Where the hell is it?*

. . . . every secret withdrawal. It's like

and propped with pillows, until I eventually fall asleep at my laptop.

I journey in my dreams to Africa, where I am minutes from the summit of Kilimanjaro. Pride courses through my veins with each cold, heavy, breathless step. As I reach the peak at Uhuru, I place a wedding photo of Brody and me on the ground, shouting my feelings to the world below. Finally, I have overcome. Finally, we are both on top of the world. I am happy again.

But just as I'm about to begin my descent, a storm blows in, and I cannot see anything. I am suddenly all alone on the top of the mountain, as cold and desperate as I've ever been, and everyone around me disappears. I scream out for help, but no one hears me. And then slowly, painfully, I freeze to death on the mountain, just like I once read about in Krakauer's book *Into Thin Air*, where people actually froze to death on the top of Mount Everest.

I wake in a full sweat, realizing that it was just a dream, and as happy as I am to realize that my dream wasn't actually real, I am

reminded of the vivid and terrifying drug-induced nightmares that
Brody used to have, right here in this same bed. I cannot get back
to sleep. One particular night pops into my mind, and I can't seem
to get the memory out of my head. In spite of his increasing hos-
tility, I continued to sleep with him in our bed, for most nights he
would just pass out and sleep into the late hours of the morning. But
on this particular night, I woke to the feeling of his hands around
my neck, choking me, begging me to get him some more pills. That
moment of being unable to breathe, the horrifying feeling that he
might actually kill me, my almost futile attempt to convince him that
he was dreaming, and that I could help him, if he'd just let go—all
of it haunts me, churning in my head. My silent prayer resulted
in the quick release of his grip, and I rolled over to cry, just as he
snapped out of his confusion to cry with me. Not too long after that,
he retreated to the bathroom for more pills. I retreated to the guest
room, thankful that the pills instantly drove him into slumber.

Now, I toss and turn again, reminded of the ill-fated journey
to Kilimanjaro in my dreams, and my ill-fated marriage to Brody.
Doubt enters my head, and I wonder if this is really what I need to
do. I don't want to die on the mountain. My soul has already died
once, right here in this house.

I cry myself to sleep, wondering if I'll ever truly be able to survive Brody's death.

39

I struggle to open my eyes. I am exhausted. *It can't possibly be morning yet*. I reach for my phone to see what time it is, but I cannot find it. I'm trying to remember where I am, confused by the fact that someone is lying next to me and disturbed by the sound of flapping nylon in heavy winds.

"Marren?" I hear Simon say through swishes of strong wind gusts. His voice seems to get vacuumed up in them. "Are you up?"

"Yes," I manage, mortified when I look over to my right to see Chris beside me. What have we done?

"Get dressed and meet us at the dining tent in fifteen minutes for breakfast before we summit," Simon says, almost screaming now over the volume of the weather.

"Okay," I say. I hope that he cannot hear the embarrassment in my voice. Even more, I hope that he doesn't discover that Chris is missing from his own tent.

I stab an elbow into Chris's midsection, and he immediately opens his eyes.

"What are you doing here?" I say. Although I don't recall anything happening between us, I can't possibly be sure. Not after the night that I couldn't remember. But then I remember that I promised him I wouldn't forget last night. Thankfully, I remember everything. *Exactly* what happened between us.

He rolls over and lets out a long morning yawn. The white scruff that has formed along the line of his jaw is turning me on.

"What time is it?" he asks, the sound of wind whipping over his gruff voice.

"I don't know. I think it must be around eleven o'clock—the time when Simon said he'd wake us."

Chris appears to gain clarity. "Oh," he says with a smile. "I guess I must have fallen asleep here."

"I guess," I say. "We didn't—"

"No, no," he says. "Of that I can be sure. I would definitely remember that, Marren. We just . . . cuddled. Please tell me that you remember too. You *promised*."

"Of course I remember. And I did promise. I remember that, too."

He smiles. The wind roars viciously outside. My stomach churns, terrified of summiting under these conditions.

"Simon said to meet in the dining tent in fifteen minutes," I say.

Chris nods at me and then peeks out of the tent, pulling back from the merciless air. "All right, see you there," he says as he ducks out of the tent, fighting with the hood of his jacket and his balaclava.

"Be careful!" I say as he disappears into the darkness.

I brave the nasty weather, praying that it doesn't blow me off the mountain. When I finally reach the dining tent, breakfast is brewing and the rest of the crew—including Chris—are conversing normally, despite the relentless, razor-sharp crackling sounds that are playing like spooky background music. Simon looks dejected. I haven't seen this kind of look on his face for the entire trip. It is somber, hesitant, dispirited. Finally, he explains why.

"Team," he says. "My duty on this journey is to get you to the summit safely. Under these conditions, I would be wrong to take you up the mountain. So tell me, can you all spare an extra day, take the time to reschedule your trips home, so that we can summit safely, at a time when the wind dies down?"

His words hit fast and hard, stealing the momentum from my

brown eyes.

Chris jumps in to answer the question first.

"I'm fine with that," he says, in his usual go-with-the-flow manner. "I can reschedule my flights and hotel reservations. I'm off for the next couple of weeks."

I suddenly wonder what to think of this. Does he actually have a job? I remember that I haven't really asked him what happened after his father died, when his brother Pete actually took over, whether he has any role in the company at all. Regardless, whatever his career situation, I am thrilled to hear that Chris can continue under Simon's revised plan.

"I'm good, too," I say. "I can reschedule everything, no problem."

True, my in-laws paid for the flights and hotels, and I know this might mean extra expenses for them. But I also know how much they love me, how grateful they are to me for the way I stayed with Brody, what it means to them for me to successfully summit this mountain. I'm certain that they would support any adjustment of plans under the circumstances. If nothing else, I'll pay for the extra expenses myself with a credit card.

Chris's face lights up at my announcement. Seri and Leslie, however, are not so happy.

Leslie purses her lips as she places an encouraging hand on Seri's. Neither of them speak. They just sit there, silent in the song of the angry wind, unable to communicate their decision.

Finally, Seri's voice commands our attention, just as it always has before.

"We will not leave this mountain until we reach the summit," she says.

Relief surges through me. They can't possibly quit now. Not this close to the top. Travel plans can be changed. But ending the climb before summiting cannot.

"We will change our plans," Seri announces.

I feel a smile spread across my face. Chris is smiling too.

But Leslie isn't smiling. "What about Janice?" she says, looking at Seri.

My smile quickly fades. I am suddenly intrigued. Who is Janice?

"Janice is Seri's mother," Leslie says. "Like Seri told you, she's battled a host of health problems throughout her life, including breast cancer. They have . . . a complicated relationship. But Seri promised to be there for her mother's surgery to remove the tumor. It's scheduled for the day after we arrive back in New Orleans. When we initially found out about the surgery, we were going to reschedule this trip. But Janice insisted that we go, because we'd be back in time."

Leslie looks at Seri again.

"We can't let her down now. We have to be there for her."

Seri's face is completely straight, devoid of emotion. And then she speaks.

"I promised Janice that I would be back for the surgery."

She exhales a long, deep breath and closes her eyes. "And I cannot break my promise. We cannot delay our return."

She takes Leslie's hand and squeezes it. I can see sorrow welling in Leslie's eyes. No one wants to make it this far, only to have to quit for reasons far beyond human control.

Simon is clearly more disturbed than Seri and Leslie combined. I can tell that he is the kind of man that wants to please his clients, wants to ensure that they enjoy a successful experience under his leadership. "I'm so sorry," he says. "I have no choice but to delay ⁱ ᵗ. Yₒᵤᵣ ₛₐfₑₜy is my very first concern. Please know that. And ... ...

that he will monitor the weather and wake us when ... ...
Seri and Leslie will spend the rest of the night here at Barafu Camp and then descend tomorrow morning. Assuming the wind dies down, it will take Chris and me an extra day to summit and get back down the mountain.

Before we go, I realize that this might be the last time I ever see Seri and Leslie. I hope not, but I can't be sure. With the wind still whipping wildly, I make sure to hug both of them, to tell them how much I enjoyed meeting them and getting to know them. We exchange contact information and promise to keep in touch. I promise that the next time I am in New Orleans, I will let them know and we will all have dinner. Kilimanjaro might have decided to alter our summiting plans, but she can never take away the friendships that have evolved on her terrain.

Chris says his goodbyes to Seri and Leslie, too, and we exit the dining tent together. He attempts to shield me from the wind, but it is no use. Conditions are unbearable. He follows me to my tent and I climb in, waiting for him to follow. Surely he will follow. But he doesn't, and I can't be quite sure why. It's so much easier to endure hardship together. I'm left alone, terrified of the elements around me, left only to pick up my copy of *Wild*, channeling some courage from Cheryl Strayed.

40

my name again, inviting me to breakfast, telling me that we are leaving for the summit within an hour.

The dining tent feels empty without Seri and Leslie, who left early to begin their descent to base camp, Simon says. Chris and I are dressed in multiple layers, puffy like giant marshmallows, ready for the kind of cold that I've never experienced. Thanks to the wind's decision to calm down, we probably won't need our balaclavas, Simon tells us, so breathing will be easier at the higher, more difficult altitudes.

As we begin our ascent, I am suddenly disappointed by the fact that headlamps aren't necessary. The sunlight has carved a beautiful path ahead, but most accounts that I have seen and read talked of summiting overnight, with headlamps that light the way—people navigating the trail like coal miners. Sadness behooves me as I accept that it's just me and Chris and Simon, in broad daylight—we will not be coal miners today.

We scramble up over small cliffs, navigating new territory. The air thins, and I find myself occasionally gasping for breath. In spite of Chris's resolve to forge ahead, Simon insists that we stop often to rest, to acclimatize, to ensure that we can properly make it to the top. *Pole, pole,* Simon reminds us as we zigzag up the switchbacks. "There is no reward for summiting quickly," he says.

During one particular rest stop, I look down to see a serpentine line of climbers making their way up too. I am hypnotized by the sight of them, suddenly wondering why each of them is here, why they would want to brave this mountain at all. As we rest quietly among the volcanic scree, I wonder the same about myself.

When I was about eight years old, I got stuck in a tree outside of our house in Clear Springs. I had climbed up high, with the fearlessness of a child, having zero awareness of the consequences. When I reached a certain point, my foot slipped, and I was forced to grab on to a high, thick branch—a hundred-year-old tree branch holding me up for dear life. Friends ran for help and my mother appeared, fresh from what I assumed to be an afternoon date with the laundry.

"Marren, sweetie," she said calmly. Another mother might likely have lost it. Called the police or fire department, perhaps. Screamed bloody murder. Not my mother. Instead, she gently coached me.

"I want you to picture something you love. Something you want more than anything. Something you would fight for. And then I want you to swing your right leg over that branch, with all of your mental might, and pull yourself to safety, so that you can climb down on your own."

Funny enough, I pictured Michael Harris's face. He was my third-grade crush, something I would fight for. Someone I wanted more than anything. I needed to save myself, so that I could have Michael. Instantly, I stopped panicking and started focusing. With all of my might, I swung a leg over the branch and inched my way back to the main trunk, easing my way down. When it was over, everyone cheered. My mother smiled. She had accomplished what every good mother hopes to accomplish: she had inspired her child to overcome adversity. To prevail over the most daunting of circumstances.

That's why I'm here, isn't it? I am here on this mountain to defeat the adversity of my past. To defeat losing Brody and my parents. To rise to the highest level of my life so far, somewhere above it all.

41

WHAT'S LEFT OF MY LIFE? The question lingers in my mind like a Rubik's cube. Despite my best efforts, I never can seem to properly resolve it.

I'm sitting at my computer—Googling Mount Kilimanjaro again—when the doorbell rings at ten in the morning, and I set my phone down next to my oversized coffee to answer it. I've poured a generous amount of dark, caffeine-laced liquid into my favorite stainless steel University of Arkansas tumbler—I'm only just beginning to feel its effects.

Just a few short years ago, coffee signified conversations with Brody—ones where we would sleep until noon after wee-hour celebrations of his many baseball victories—mornings when the light of day would rouse him and he would reach over and make sweet love to me and we'd lie in bed together, our bodies one, until one of us would get hungry and demand a lunchtime breakfast. That's when the coffee would come, along with Brody's signature eggs and bacon (the only thing he could actually cook) at one thirty in the afternoon on a random Sunday. Those were the days.

The doorbell rings again. Slightly jittery from the caffeine, I make my way to the front door and peer through the mail slot, wondering who it could be. When I see his familiar eyes, the brilliant hazel-green ones, I smile to myself. Something about his arrival has made me feel better, less alone. There is still someone that cares enough to show up and check on me today.

I unlock the door and invite him in.

"George," I say. "I'm so happy you're here."

He gives me a proper hug and makes a beeline for the couch. ˙˙ ˙˙ ˙ ˙˙˙˙ ˙ˋ˙˙˙ he strategically arranges himself, just before he

you in anything that you decide to do, from this point on..

No mention of Greta, thankfully. His words coerce me. *Tell him. Tell him what it is that you want to do.*

"Thank you, George. And if you're serious," I say, "I'd like to ask your opinion on something."

"Anything," he says, his eyes fixed sharply on mine.

"I want to climb a mountain. Brody told me to do it. In my dream."

George looks absolutely mystified. He furrows his brow and squints his eyes in obvious concern.

"I want to climb Mount Kilimanjaro. And I want your blessing— yours and Trish's."

He doesn't respond.

"It's what I need to do," I say.

George is quiet, and his silence is defeating. I can tell from his expression that he doesn't know quite what to say. I know he wants me to be happy, but I can see doubt blooming in his eyes. Climbing a mountain is obviously not the kind of happiness that he wants for me.

In spite of his hesitance, he agrees to look at some websites about Kilimanjaro. I pull up some of my favorites. The pictures are breathtaking, and they seem to pique George's interest in a way that I hoped they would. I click on picture after picture. The brilliant hues of green forest decorated with distant, snow-capped land rising into the clouds seem to hypnotize him. He stands next to me, perfectly still, clearly interested in seeing more.

I stop clicking and turn to George, wanting to secure his approval. I need someone to validate my idea of doing this, someone to care enough to support my journey to a destination far beyond my comfort zone.

"Are you sure this is what you want?" he asks.

"Yes," I tell him. "I am positive." Actually I'm not, but I want him to think I am.

"But it's dangerous. Brody wouldn't want you to be in danger. He loved you so much."

I'm not sure what comes over me, but George's words leave me bitter. Livid.

"Really, George? Is that what you think? He loved me so much that he ruined our whole life together with his drug habit? That he squandered all of the money my parents left me on his pills? That he left me with no life insurance and a bank account that might last me a couple of months at best? That's *love*? I think not."

George looks down and shakes his head. He cannot disagree. Finally, he speaks.

"All right, dear. If this is how you feel, then at least let me help. If you are so insistent on climbing this mountain, then let's get you there in style. I'll pay for your plane ticket, business class on the airline of your choice."

His words ignite flames of ambition inside of me. I smile. We hug. My favorite wedding picture with Brody, neatly framed in weathered wood on a living room shelf across the room from us, glistens in the sunlight coming in through a side window.

I envision vials of hydrocodone, me dumping them down the side of a mountain, watching each pill as it falls to its own death. The thought of this invigorates me. It is freeing, encouraging, summoning me to take action.

42

AFTER OUR REST STOP, the sparse vegetation that once surrounded us is replaced by snow. At zero degrees, the cold is intolerable up here. A mild wind—thankfully not as intense as the wind last night—makes the temperature feel more like fifteen below. I secure my balaclava as scenes from *Into Thin Air* continue to flash through my mind, and every cell in my body begs me to turn back. My teeth chatter; my hands and feet are numb. I fear the worst—hypothermia, high-altitude cerebral edema, or high-altitude pulmonary edema—as my body revolts against the excruciatingly high altitude and scary temperatures.

You cannot do this. Turn back now, Marren.

Chris follows closely behind me, a safety net of sorts. His presence is pushing me forward. I don't want to disappoint him. I don't want to disappoint Simon. And I most certainly don't want to disappoint my mother, whose voice echoes in my mind, telling me to think of something that I loved, something I would fight for, someone who inspired me to dig deep and persevere.

That someone used to be Brody. Now, I'm thinking of someone else.

"Are you okay?" Chris asks.

The cold makes even the simplest of tasks—like turning around to answer a question—even harder. I cannot feel my hands. I cannot feel my feet. And even though my lips are practically frozen together, I manage to say the words.

"I am. Because of you."

▲ ▲ ▲

Stella Point—one of three potential summit

Simon brings

shoulder. I pull down my balaclava and bring the steaming liquid slowly to my lips, savoring its warmth as I take a long, drawn-out sip. My body instantly thaws a bit; I am ever so grateful.

Chris walks over to me, his face splotchy and red with windburn, and offers me his hand. We stand on the edge of a snowy crater together, admiring the scenic view. Chris snaps a few pictures as Simon points out that the remainder of our journey will involve a snow-covered ridgeline, which, though seemingly short and simple, will be somewhat complicated by adverse conditions.

"Get ready," he says. "What seems like a walk in the park will become a marathon."

Great.

Our final destination is still about an hour and a half away, Simon explains. The wind is getting worse, and in spite of my mental stamina, I am overcome with emotion as I watch those who have already ascended as they make their descent. They pass by us, waving, wishing us luck, giving us the thumbs-up, telling us that we can do this—just like *they* did. To me, these climbers are rock stars. Mentors who have mastered the challenge that I am about to undertake. I am inspired by their energy.

I think back to everything it's taken to get here.

The weeks of training, pummeling my body like a boxing opponent. Three-mile runs, then four-mile runs, and eventually six-mile runs, three times a week. On days that I didn't run, I'd hit the treadmill, set on an incline of 12.0, for thirty minutes at a time. Painful repetitions of lunges, squats, sit ups, and leg curls. Hours of climbing the bleachers at the Clear Springs High School football stadium.

I once read that climbing Kilimanjaro was simply one long, strenuous hike, so I began to climb up and down the stadium bleachers carrying twenty pounds of free weights in a backpack, four times a week, wearing the same pair of Asolo hiking boots that every single article I'd ever read on climbing Kilimanjaro had warned me to "break in" before my trip.

On one particularly warm, sticky afternoon in late spring, as the dogwoods were blooming all over south Arkansas, I ran swiftly to the top of the stadium, not losing breath or focus, and when I reached the very top, I didn't want to come down. I stood on the highest bleacher, looking out at the horizon, admiring a deep, powder-blue sky that spanned the distance. Sweat was beading on my forehead as the memory of Brody and all of his baseball prowess came to me. The sky reminded me of his infinite potential. But I was the athlete now. I was the one who needed to succeed. There was no scholarship at stake, no scouts touting my talent. Just me and my desire to climb a mountain.

And now here I am—just a girl from little Clear Springs, Arkansas—about to reach the top of Kilimanjaro.

I can't believe how far I've come.

43

never traveled —

off champagne and sleeping horizontally on a plane makes me smile. At over thirty-five hours of total travel time, it won't be a short trip—nevertheless, I can't wait.

As excited as I am, Brody is still everywhere. In my mind, in this house. Everywhere. The smell of his Tom Ford cologne—a distinct mixture of fig, truffle, and cedarwood—looms all around me. It's in the air, in the dress shirts and sport coats that still hang in his closet, in the chair where he would sit to peruse his iPad every night. Here, I cannot escape it.

Soon, however, I will breathe in the fresh scent of trees and land. I will inhale crisp, clean air laced with the smell of unique vegetation that I've never seen. I will catch a breeze coming down off the snow-capped mountains in the distance, and then I will be up there, right in the midst of that breeze.

I study my computer screen. The Out Yonder website tells me exactly what I'll need for the trip. A good (i.e., expensive) sleeping bag. A pillow. An air mattress. A daypack with essentials like water, snacks, a camera, toilet paper, toiletries, and extra clothing. So many brands, so many decisions to make. I scrutinize the reviews and gamble on my choices, hoping that the input from others will lead me to the best products.

▲ ▲ ▲

Three days to go. I stare at the equipment in front of me, which I have zealously collected and prepared: a Mountain Hardware sleeping bag, synthetic and cocoon-like, rated for zero degrees; a Sea to Summit air mattress, celebrated on Amazon for its extraordinary comfort and insulation from the harsh ground; a Klymit pillow, firm enough to support an exhausted head and yet lightweight enough to tote on a mountain trek; and an Arc'teryx backpack, light and durable enough to carry essentials.

Thank you, Amazon.

My flight is less than seventy-two hours away, and butterflies flitter in my stomach as I study my passport. Just a few weeks ago, this trip was merely a thought inside my head, a coping mechanism to deal with my husband's untimely departure from this world. Now, it is a reality. Soon, I will be on a plane, headed for a kind of journey that I've never attempted to undertake. My gut cinches at the thought of arriving in Tanzania alone, for I have never even been off of U.S. soil.

My phone rings, and I look down to see who it is.

George. I pick it up, excited to share my feelings about the trip with him.

"Marren," he says. "Are you free tomorrow night? There's something else we'd like to give you before you leave."

I stare at my climbing equipment again, wondering what more he has in store. The business-class flight to Kilimanjaro was more than enough.

"I'm completely free," I say. "What's going on?"

"Trish and I would like to host a going away party of sorts," he says. "To give you a proper send-off to your mountain adventure."

A giant smile spreads across my face. "Thank you, George," I tell him. "And Trish. You have been so kind to me. I'll never forget how kind you've been to me. It's meant the world."

George doesn't speak. But then he does.

"We will always love you." Another brief silence. "And I'm just sorry the drugs couldn't allow Brody to do the same."

I'm not sure how to respond.

The "going away" party is at George and Trish's house. It is decorated beautifully, in the same French country theme as the house she redecorated for us on Quiet Oaks Lane. An antique hutch resides in the dining room—doused in a weathered French gray—holding ivory dishes and tiny topiaries in its delicate grip. Two-paneled, arched mirrors hang symmetrically below distressed wooden beams atop the high ceiling in the giant, open living room, where two settees are perched across from each other, divided by a large wooden coffee table with beautifully carved legs that bulge out like a spider's. Stone floors and raw wood give the place a rustic feel.

Trish's favorite ceramic chicken watches us as we gather in the kitchen around a mountain-shaped cake that wishes me well.

"Good Luck, Marren!" it says in scripted red icing.

I sip a crystal glass of champagne as I stare at the small group of well-wishers around me. Brody's best friends from grade school,

Jay Bradford and Mark Lewis—fellow baseball players who, in spite of Brody's struggle with hydrocodone, never abandoned the friendship. And Brody's parents, of course. And, to my surprise, Molly.

▲ ▲ ▲

There is an obvious discomfort between Molly and me, because we haven't spoken in so long. I think of her sweet text after the funeral and the way I ignored it. I hope she will forgive me. It was nice of George and Trish to include her, to try and bring us all back together again this way. I shoot a nervous look her way, but she just smiles the same old Molly smile, an expression that whispers, "I'm here for you, no matter what."

George raises a toast, and we all drink to my endeavor. He hands me a package that is gorgeously packaged in butcher paper with rainbow-colored ribbon. "The colors of celebration," Trish says. "Brody is cheering for you in heaven."

I feel a smile radiate across my face. The sound of his name still pains me, but I am grateful for these sweet people, the kind of people who are trying hard to make beauty from ashes.

I tear open the package and find a beautiful journal. It is covered in a soft, supple brown leather and filled with handmade, deckle-edged vintage paper—made by a company called Nomad Crafts. I trace a finger along the outside of it and stare at it in awe. It is like feeling a weathered piece of silk.

"We want you to write about your journey," George says. "So that you can remember it forever."

I am so humbled that words won't come.

George delivers something else to me, a card encased in a mountain-brown envelope. I tear it open and begin to read. Inside, there are several small but mighty messages:

You've got this, Marren!

Go, Marren!

Thinking of you and wishing you all the best in your amazing journey.

The words lift me to new heights. I am suddenly more determined than ever. I place the card on the table as the tears fall from my grateful eyes.

"Thank you so much, everyone. I can't tell you what this means to me. You all have been so good to me and Bro—" I stop before I can say his name out loud. "You all have been so good to me," I correct myself.

̂ ̇ ̇ ̇ ̇ of mountain cake. "You are the

44

THE RIDGELINE TO UHURU PEAK is just as Simon described it. A walk in the park that feels like a marathon. I am on mile twenty-three, ready to give up. My legs are bricks, my body a frozen statue. I struggle for breath. If not for my balaclava, my tears would turn into icicles.

I can't do this.

In spite of my passion for running, there's a reason I have never actually run a marathon. Though Brody once encouraged me, I always dismissed him. A marathon was too much, I'd tell myself. There was a chance I wouldn't finish. Two or three or four miles at a time were no big deal. I could always finish a short run. It invigorated me—gave me the kind of high that I supposed Brody was getting from the drugs. But a long run was different. It would be daunting, draining. Just like much of my life with Brody. I didn't know if I had what it took to endure it. Fearing failure, I never tried.

Now, I start to feel the same way. I don't want to fail, so I don't want to try.

"I can't do this anymore," I say to Chris, the cold piercing through the layers of my clothing like sharp icicles. I attempt to turn around and go back, but Chris stops me.

"I won't let you go. Please don't give up on me now."

They are the same words that Brody said to me, again and again: *Please don't give up on me now.* I didn't give up then, and I can't give up now. I must persevere, endure, push myself beyond my limits to find success this time around.

I hike the last few meters, lost in my own feelings. The tempera- and the wind is gusting up

ding day, devastated by the aisle. The night Brody hit me, when I was humiliated in front of Dr. C in the emergency room. Brody's funeral, when I was left alone with a life in ruins. Now, the fresh hell of this ruthless mountain.

Just a few feet to go.

One step. Then another. Finally, I am here. The wooden sign with the words "Uhuru Peak"—the roof of Africa—etched in a weathered yellow, appears before me. I have officially summited Kilimanjaro. I drop down to my knees, grabbing handfuls of volcanic rock, just like William the Conqueror did in 1066 when he fell onto the sand after landing in England and said, "Look, I have conquered England with both hands."

Look, Mom and Dad. Look, Brody. Look, Chris. I have conquered my past with both hands.

At last, I am free, vindicated by my fierce determination. I pull my balaclava down and shout it to the world: "I did it!"

177

I feel Chris's arms around me, and before I know it, he pulls me to my feet and presses his sweet, thick lips to mine. Simon takes our picture. This precious moment, made even more so by being kissed at 19,341 feet by a man that I am growing to need more each day, is forever captured in the digital world.

Chris's kiss ignites a new self-confidence within me, reminding me what I have accomplished. The rocks in my pocket whisper their congratulations—they are silent cheerleaders, encouraging me on to a life after Brody in Clear Springs. *If you can summit Kilimanjaro, you can do anything*, they tell me.

Simon takes more pictures, and so does Chris. I am amazed by the way they are able to remove their gloves for this purpose—my fingers are so cold and numb now that I can't bear to try and move them. Chris places his iPhone in front of me and takes a selfie of the two of us. Our smiles are full of perseverance.

I can't remember the last time I felt this good about myself.

▲ ▲ ▲

Just fifteen minutes later, we begin our descent to Barafu Camp.

Chris throws his arm around my shoulder, reminding me how proud he is of our accomplishment.

"Way to go, Mare," he says. "I'm proud of you."

I smile.

"Thanks," I say. "I'm proud of me too."

We continue the path down the mountain, across the same volcanic wasteland that we braved on the way up. The cold that once ailed me is more tolerable now, thanks to the adrenaline rush of reaching Uhuru. I take out my trekking poles, relishing the breathtaking views of long marsh and snowy, white patches in the distance. Something that feels like happiness dances around in my soul.

With each step down, I can feel the oxygen returning to my lungs. "It will be slippery," Simon says, "full of loose gray rocks known as volcanic scree."

Chris has obviously navigated terrain like this somewhere before, because he glides down like a skilled skier. I, on the other hand, am not so skilled. Even with trekking poles, I take a few steps and lose my balance, tumbling to the ground screaming. Thankfully, I land on my bottom. I am uninjured yet mortified. To make matters worse, Chris is laughing from a distance. I want to punch him.

offers some helpful tips on

then he slides down carefully, like a mountain snowboarder.

"The key is to slide," he says. "Sliding is much better and faster than walking. Look for areas with smaller stones—they are easier to slide on. Lean your weight into the pole."

He ends his on-site lesson as he slides to a beautiful halt, about twenty-five feet below me.

I throw one of my poles downhill, and it tumbles to Simon. Imitating his instructions as best I can, I position myself in a parallel manner and brace with a single pole. I push off, suddenly feeling like a surfer riding some sort of rocky wave. Before I know it, I am next to Simon, and he is smiling.

"That's the way, Marren," he says.

I push off again, deciding that this part can be fun if I let it. Soon I am close to Chris, and he laughs as I ride my alpine surfboard toward him. Finally, I slide in beside him.

"Took you a while, huh?"

I take a trekking pole and pretend to whack him in the head. Simon tells us to look up so that we can see the summit at Uhuru again. Tiny humans are crawling like ants on the top. We've made good progress.

When we resume our descent, my knees begin to ache. They are incredibly sore, battered by the challenge of these past few days. In desperate need of rest, I'm hopeful that we're not far from Barafu Camp. Due to our unexpected wind delay, we will stay there again tonight, then make our way to Mweka Camp tomorrow morning.

45

Simon ge... ..., ...
another expedition crew. They're a miracle cure for knee pain, he
assures me. I am hesitant, but trust Simon's advice. After all, he has
led us safely up to the top of Mount Kilimanjaro and back. Why
should I doubt him now?

I take the patches back to my tent and affix one to each knee. I
find my copy of *Wild* and dive back into it, high on the energy from
today's victory.

The patches help. I still don't know what's in them, but whatever it is works beautifully. I can walk much more easily now, and
the pain has gone from a level eight to a level two. I can handle level
two discomfort. It's a small price to pay for the exhilarating experience I've enjoyed here.

Tonight is our last dinner on the mountain. There is much to celebrate. "The *real* celebration will occur tomorrow at Mweka Camp,"
Simon tells us. "We'll all feel much better after a good night's rest."

Dinner is our best yet. Small beef steaks and potatoes, green beans, and a fabulous, brownie-like dessert. I indulge in a glass of wine while Chris nurses a beer. We are high on achievement and alcohol, basking in the camaraderie that has led us here tonight. I feel so good that I almost request another glass of wine, but I convince myself that it isn't a good idea.

According to Simon, we have to be up early tomorrow for the final trek to Mweka Camp and the Mweka Gate. "So don't stay up late!" he warns. Nevertheless, Chris celebrates after dinner with a group of South African climbers who, like us, decided to summit midday due to the wind. They are a particularly rowdy, the-more-the-merrier type of crowd.

I have mentally deemed one of them as the "ringleader," because of his deep, commanding voice and the way that he constantly barks out instructions. He has long blond hair and piercing blue eyes, with a body that could easily take a place on the cover of *GQ*. Seeing him and Chris and the rest of the South African crew singing and dancing together is any girl's dream—such handsome men in such a beautifully rugged setting, living out pure fun, celebrating an admirable accomplishment.

"Get me another beer!" they all chant together. "Come on, over here! Cheers to us, tonight we make a ruckus!"

As I'm watching, Chris waves me over, beckoning for me to join them. But I am much too tired. I heed Simon's warning, choosing to retire to Old Red alone, where I decide to journal until sleep takes over.

46

mother's mother ...

special days when I got to spend the night with her. I can picture her hair, done up perfectly into a small bun on top of her head as she stood wearing a frilly apron in her timeless kitchen. I always loved her breakfasts, especially because she took the time to special-make my scrambled eggs. No bacon grease, lots of butter. I imagine a plate of fluffy yellow scrumptiousness in front of me, remembering how that first bite would always melt deliciously in my mouth, followed by the crunchy goodness of her oven-cooked bacon. Less mess to cook it in the oven, she once explained. Easy cleanup. Because of my Memaw, I've never cooked bacon on the stovetop in my life.

Her bacon and eggs were delicious, but the best part of breakfast at Memaw's was that she let me have a cup of coffee with her, as early as age six.

"Don't tell your mother," she'd say. And I wouldn't. Another smell—fresh coffee brewing—is once again coaxing me out of Old Red now.

For one last time, I get dressed and head to the dining tent, where I'm overcome by sadness, a sense of mourning for the loss of the rest of our crew. I miss Leslie's sweet voice and Seri's confidence. I wonder where they are and what they are doing right now. I wonder how leaving early made them feel. I wonder if they will ever try to summit Kilimanjaro again, and what they would say if they knew we finally made it yesterday. And I am guessing they do know, and it feels awful.

Chris is already at the table, studying his copy of *Lonesome Dove*. He looks up at me as I enter and smiles.

"Well, hey there, sleepyhead," he says. "You zonked out early last night, didn't you?"

I can't believe how chipper he is, given that it is so early. I'd bet good money that he stayed up well into the wee hours last night.

"I was so tired," I say.

"Today will be easier," Simon says as he douses a piece of toast in strawberry jam. "A three-hour trip to the Mweka Camp, where we will stop for a quick lunch, then on to the Mweka Gate, about another two and a half hours. From there, we'll get back to Arusha for a late dinner. I asked my people to rebook your hotel and flight arrangements, Marren."

I look at Chris, who is sipping coffee as he's reading. It suddenly hits me that our time together will soon be over.

"What about Chris?" I say.

His eyes dart over to me. "Me?" he asks.

I nod.

"I've decided to stay longer—for a safari," he says. "I hadn't originally planned to do it, but Simon convinced me. I mean, when in Tanzania . . ." He laughs, as does Simon.

"You're scheduled to fly back late tomorrow night," Simon says to me. "The airline was very nice. No change fee. They even found you a spot in business class!"

184

Chris smiles at this. "Oh, *I see*. You're a princess, eh?"

I can feel myself blushing. I wonder what he'd say if I told him that my dead husband's parents were paying for all of this. I also wonder what George and Trish would think of Chris.

I wish I *was* a princess. Maybe then my fairy tale would have actually come true.

▲ ▲ ▲

...th ...armer windy conditions. Given

we encounter ...g

Though I don't intend to eavesdrop, I can overhear Chris and Simon as they converse about Chris's safari plans. I can't help listening to what they say.

Simon describes the wildlife that Chris is sure to see, along with the pictures he is certain to capture. The Serengeti is home to some of the world's most beautiful creatures, Simon explains, assuring Chris that he is sure to see animals like zebras, lions, wildebeest, impala, buffalo, giraffes, kudu, and elephants along the way.

"A Tanzanian safari is no ordinary vacation," Simon says.

"Good," Chris replies. "Because I like extraordinary things."

In all of my research on climbing Kilimanjaro, I came across numerous websites that advertised safaris as a post-Kilimanjaro option. The images I saw were some of the most fascinating I'd ever come across. Truthfully, if I'd had the money, I would have signed up for one of these safaris too. I swallow hard, trying to keep my jealousy at bay. Because my journey will end at the hotel in Arusha,

I won't get to witness the full spectrum of everything that Tanzania has to offer before I go.

Poor Marren. I am reminded of the way that Brody used to taunt me.

Poor Marren, he'd say. *You don't get a professional baseball player who makes millions. Poor Marren, stuck here in small-town Arkansas instead of big-city bliss. Poor Marren, chained to the life she always wanted to escape. Poor Marren, always the victim.*

I can't listen to Brody speak to me that way anymore. Never again will his addiction steal my joy. I am *not* a victim. I am victorious.

Finally.

47

prepare

the porters have a special surprise for

of me as the members of our crew line up outside of the dining tent, hand in hand. Simon gives me a sheet of paper with a bunch of words printed on it. Suddenly, the crew belts out in song. It's a beautiful chorus that begins with "Jambo," but after that I don't understand anything because it's in Swahili.

I study the sheet paper that Simon gave me. The lyrics are typed in both Swahili and English, and I try to follow along. It's called the "Kilimanjaro Song," and it's about welcoming guests to the mountain and encouraging them to drink plenty of water and something about watching as the mountain wraps around them like a snake.

Simon explains that this is a farewell song sung by expeditions after a successful trek up the mountain and back. The crew sings it over and over, dancing and cheering, inviting Chris and me to join. Once again, Chris drags me into the spotlight, and we clap and sway and gyrate together, paying our respects to these wonderful men who have made it possible for us to accomplish such a formidable goal.

When the song is done, we pack up for the very last time and begin our three-hour journey to the Mweka Gate. We follow a scarped, sidewalk-like trail with abundant vegetation, including twenty-foot-tall fern trees that remind me of something prehistoric. As we press on, I feel tiny droplets of water against my skin, a slight drizzle. A light fog envelops us. In spite of the dreary conditions, I am thrilled to be back in the rainforest. The plant life here is some of the most fascinating I've ever seen. I smile as I reach down to touch a dew-covered *Impatiens kilimanjari*, remembering—as if it was already so long ago—the first one I saw on our way up the mountain. It whispers to me in bright red words, the same rich color of its petals, "You did it, Marren. Good job."

At one point, Simon stops us, insisting that we look back to catch one last magnificent view of Kilimanjaro. I admire her from a distance, grateful for the chance to have known her so intimately.

Asante, Kilimanjaro. Thank you for the chance to feel alive again.

Eventually, we reach steps that are littered with treacherous roots, the size of which might trip you up if you aren't careful. *Pole, pole,* Simon reminds us. It is here—at the very end of the journey—that many climbers get complacent and often unnecessarily injured, he says.

We are minutes from the Mweka Gate now. The rain has stopped, and we come to a particularly beautiful area with a high canopy of trees and an open-air feel. I look up to see blue sky, along with something that I will never, ever forget—a beautiful rainbow overhead, the most befitting of endings to this adventure. For the short duration of the trek, I hum the tune to Kacey Musgraves's "Rainbow" to myself. My heart is in a beautiful new place, right here, under this rainbow.

▲ ▲ ▲

At the Mweka Gate, our small group of porters awaits with a celebratory cake. "Congratulations!" is written neatly in green across the top.

They've set up a single tent to celebrate our journey, and we feast on spongy yellow goodness as they serenade us with the "Kilimanjaro" song once again. They dance and chant and laud our accomplishment—Chris appears to be in heaven, while I turn ... with embarrassment.

you here today has been critical in making a dream come true for us. Right, Marren?"

He looks at me, waiting for an answer. I nod enthusiastically.

"So it's with great pleasure that we leave you with this, a special gift to express our sincere appreciation. A tip that Simon will distribute equally among you all. *Asante!*"

With that, our time on the mountain is officially done.

48

TWO AND A HALF HOURS LATER, we are back in Arusha, a late dinner awaiting us. Nestled in a small chair across from Chris and Simon, I finish a glass of wine and then allow myself to order a second one.

Just this once.

Already three beers in, Chris is in full storytelling mode. He recounts some memorable moments from our trip: Casey and Claire's T-shirts, my panic attack on the Barranco Wall, my tumble down the slippery scree, and finally, Simon's picture of our kiss at Uhuru Peak.

"Were you surprised?" he asks me. "I hope so. Because I'm good at surprises."

My eyes immediately widen, and I squirm a little as the entire table erupts in laughter. I can tell that he sees this as fun. My face begins to burn—I can feel the redness settling in just before my second glass of wine arrives. *Perfect timing.* I take a sip, hoping that we'll move quickly past this uncomfortable subject. I do not actually answer his question.

Chris and Simon take turns sharing more stories, and an abundance of laughter ensues. I finish my second glass of wine, which I begin to regret, because alcohol never fails to conjure up old emotions. Memories of the mountain start to flood my mind. I think of Casey and Claire, of that harrowing moment when Claire couldn't breathe, the urgency in Seri's voice when she listened to Claire's lungs. I picture the look on Seri's face when the wind delayed our summit, how her eyes weighed the decision to support her mother. And, of course, I feel Chris's lips on mine again, knowing that, but

̄ ̄ ̣ ̄ of us, I might never see his face again. It's like our

must think I am.

Halfway through glass number three, I get personal. "I don't want to go home," I say, the alcohol fighting away tears.

"Neither do I," Chris says. "Let's stay forever. Climb Kili over and over again." His hand finds mine as he laughs at his own words as he takes another drink. Euphoria sprouts through me. We're officially holding hands.

"I'm serious," I say, squeezing my fingers into his.

"Me too," he says, squeezing back, still laughing.

"No, really. I can't go back. I can't face the lawsuit. It's too much."

Suddenly, his grip goes limp, and he removes his hand from mine. His once-jovial eyes are cold, and his entire body shuts down mid-laugh. The expression on his face resembles the look. The same one that George wears when he dares to broach the hardest of topics.

Chris sets his drink down. His version of the look commands my attention.

"Marren," he begins. "There is something I . . . something that . . . well, look, I just *really* don't want to talk about this."

"About what?"

He crinkles his nose and shakes his head.

"About the lawsuit," he begins. "I just *can't*. I'm sorry. I'm not the right person for this conversation. And on that note, I want to be clear. I like you. I really do. But now . . . I'm thinking that it's just not the right time for us."

A strange combination of disappointment and fury invades me. I am beyond offended. He doesn't want to talk about it? Am I bothering him with my problems? He doesn't want to at least *try* to help me? And perhaps the worst . . . *it's just not the right time for us?*

Wow.

"Fine, then," I say. "So long, Chris."

I storm off to my room.

I never want to see Chris Courtland again.

49

off my iPhone alarm, remembering Chris's crushing words.

It's just not the right time for us.

A stinging sensation rips through me. I open my eyes, and the sunlight sears into them as the flashbacks of last night begin. I cringe as I think of the way I stormed off like a kid. I knew I shouldn't have ordered that third glass of wine.

I grab my phone off the nightstand. No texts, no calls, no sign of any communication from Chris. A dull pain arises in my chest.

Should I try to call him?

But then I realize that I don't have his number, because we haven't had any reason to communicate by phone.

Should I stop by his room? I pop up from the bed and quickly shower and dress, frantically trying to decide my course of action. As I'm flat-ironing my hair, I look down at my phone to see a green text box appear. My heart is hopeful, but instantly sinks when I see that it is a reminder from the airline about my flight.

I pack up my things and head out the door, wondering if I should just go straight to his room. Then I realize that I don't even remember which room he's in. He didn't tell me last night. I didn't give him a chance to tell me. So I head for the lobby, praying that the front desk attendant will share Chris's room number with me.

Back home in the United States, no one would dare give out such information without proper vetting. But here in this Tanzanian hotel, where the rules seem much more relaxed, I am hopeful that I can more easily obtain it. So I stroll up to the front desk, showered and fresh with styled hair for the first time in more than a week, and I smile.

"I need a favor," I say. "I'm leaving to return home to the United States today, and I need to say goodbye to my friend, who is staying here for a safari. We just summited Kilimanjaro together. Can you possibly give me his room number so I can tell him goodbye before he leaves? His name is Chris Courtland."

To my delight, the front desk clerk—a friendly, bald Tanzanian whose nametag reads "Akida"—types something into the computer. Hope whirls around in my stomach, but Akida shakes his head.

"I'm sorry, madam, but Mr. Courtland checked out earlier this morning. I believe he had an early departure for his safari trip."

I am robbed of hope, powerless, in utter disbelief that this is how it actually ends. I feel like Bridget Jones in the final part of *Bridget Jones's Diary*—the scene where she finds out that Mark Darcy is moving from London to New York—and there's not a damn thing she can do about it.

I thank the front desk clerk and take a dispirited seat in the hotel lobby, wondering if I should try to call Chris—knowing that wherever he is, there likely won't be any service. The pit in my stomach is expanding rapidly. There is nothing I can do, except ask Akida to call me a cab for the airport.

I pull out my copy of *Wild*, my bags sitting at my feet, and I wait an hour for the taxi to pick me up. I devour the pages, and I am no longer Bridget Jones. I'm Cheryl Strayed, completing a solo journey along the Pacific Coast Trail. When the taxi arrives, I put away the book and take a long, slow, deep breath. I am once again Marren Halleck, the girl who lost her husband to addiction, the same one who seems to have just lost her chance with Chris Courtland.

But I am the girl I came here to be, right? The girl who can survive on her own.

50

THE FLIGHT FROM KILIMANJARO National Airport to Doha is smooth and uneventful, except for the firestorm of thoughts I'm having about Chris. The way his hands felt when he was teaching me how to use the camera. His masculine, leathery smell in the tent on the night before we summited. And of course, the surprise kiss, followed by the deflating "now isn't the time" speech. Another long layover in the Doha airport means more time in the fantastic lounge there to ponder what went wrong. After studying Facebook and Twitter and Instagram ad nauseam and practically drowning myself in water (hydration is key!), I conk out in a chair.

When I wake, my neck is stiff. It takes me a minute to remember where I am. *Ah, yes. I'm in the Doha airport lounge. Did I oversleep? Miss my next flight?* My pulse races, and confusion nags me. I am groggy and unmotivated. Clearly, something has me down.

It's Chris. I can't get him out of my head.

I sprawl out on a small sofa in the Doha airport lounge, grateful for good Wi-Fi. Boredom commands me to scroll through my Facebook feed. The taste of champagne and orange juice sizzles on my tongue as I take a sip of mimosa and study the collection of photos on my phone, contemplating exactly which ones to post.

Most of them include Chris.

There it is again, that dull ache in my chest. I search for Chris on Facebook. Perhaps he'll accept my friend request if I make one. I then remember that he's on safari and won't have internet access for a while. I search for him anyway.

"Chris Courtland," I type. But none of the results that turn up are him. More chest pain. Another sip of my drink helps to combat it, but I need something more. I pull my journal and a pen from my carry-on and begin to scribble away, thinking back to my last few

i· R... J.. On the narticularly hard days, I would write

can't. So I write and endure. And I say the serenity prayer w ..., again and again, just like I used to in the worst of times with Brody.

God grant me the serenity to accept the things I cannot change, the courage to change the things that I can, and the wisdom to know the difference.

I hope the words are enough. Somehow, I doubt they will be.

▲ ▲ ▲

The flight attendant delivers a lovely glass of champagne before take-off, but I refuse it. As I study the fancy champagne flute in her hands, I think of Brody, and I wonder what might have been if addiction hadn't stolen him away. Could we have been on this plane together, enjoying a moderate dose of pre-flight champagne? Would he have been up to conquering Mount Kilimanjaro too?

Guilt seeps into my soul. I must stop obsessing about Chris. My heart will forever belong to Brody.

Or maybe it won't.

As the plane ascends, I can't shake off my thoughts of Chris. He was supposed to be my way forward. The chemistry between us was supposed to propel me into bold new places. I cannot let what we shared on that mountain go. Not without a fight. As we bounce around in the air, rising to our cruising altitude, I have an idea.

I take out my phone and I begin to type an email. I know I cannot send it until we land, but it feels good to try and tell Chris how I'm feeling right now. I picture him standing on the mountain, taking one of what must have been a thousand pictures, sweat sliding down his tanned skin as he reaches to adjust his Tilley hat. I see him turn to smile at me—*Marren from Arkansas.*

It can't end this way. It just can't.

My fingers fly all over the keyboard on my phone screen as the feelings scramble out of me, fresh and raw like the yolk of an egg. Finally, after multiple revisions, I finish the message to Chris. It reads as follows:

Dear Chris,

I don't really know what to say, other than I'm sorry. Sorry that things ended the way they did. Sorry that I acted like a five-year-old. Sorry that we didn't get the chance to say a proper goodbye. I guess in a way, I agree that now isn't a good time for us, whatever "us" means. But I can't rule out the possibility that someday, the time may be just right. Anyway, I am forever grateful that I met you and for the way you championed me to the top of that mountain.

Thank you for showing me what it's like to be passionate about something—and someone—again.

All the best,
Marren

I copy Chris's email address from one of Simon's messages and insert it after "To." But I do not hit send. Instead, I save it as a draft.

51

ALMOST SIXTEEN HOURS LATER, we land in Houston.

A trace of sadness creeps into me as the wheels of the Boeing 777 hit the pavement. On one hand, it's good to be home. I've missed familiar soil, the protective layer of routine. But on the other, I am lured away by Chris's words again.

Marren from Arkansas.

His deep voice lingers in my head, satiating my thoughts, summoning me back to the mountain with Simon and friends. Every time I hear him speak, I long to be somewhere far away from here again, together with Chris, ready to take on something exciting and new. There is nothing new and exciting about life in Clear Springs.

As we pull into the gate, I take out my phone and pull up the email to Chris. I study the message I've written, wondering what Chris might say if he could read it. As the plane comes to a stop and the people around me begin to gather their things, I attempt to click into my actual inbox. But when I do, my finger fumbles, and I accidentally hit send.

Oh. My. God. I *sent* it to him. He will actually see it now.

Oh, no. What have I done?

▲ ▲ ▲

I face a six-hour drive home from Houston's George W. Bush Intercontinental Airport to Clear Springs. Plagued with worry over the accidental email, I plug in my phone and pull up one of my favorite playlists, which I have labeled as "Kili trip." Toto's "Africa" resounds through my car as I picture Kilimanjaro in the distance, a nice distraction from the dull sight of incessant asphalt ahead. I check my phone often, but there is still no response from Chris. He is still on safari, I remind myself. Probably without internet for days.

The drive-through line is long, but I wait in it anyway. As I finally get to the window, the curly-headed teenager who is working there hands me a greasy brown bag. I dive into the cheeseburger and large order of fries, thinking of the dining tent and the food that we enjoyed each night on the mountain. It almost seems surreal now. Just a few days ago, I summited Mount Kilimanjaro with Chris, and now I'm here alone, wiping a dollop of ketchup from my mouth as I scarf down a McDonald's cheeseburger.

Life is an interesting creature. A chameleon that can rapidly change colors.

As I'm swallowing the last bite of my juicy cheeseburger, it hits me. That's me. I'm a chameleon, changing colors, slowly but surely finding my own strength to keep up with this ever-changing thing called life.

▲ ▲ ▲

George, Trish, and Molly are standing in my driveway when I arrive home. They are holding up signs that say "Congratulations!" and "Welcome Home!" I feel blessed, struck once again by the fact that Brody's parents have always been the parents I never got to have, once the accident took them away. The people that are here have known me all of my life.

Trish has ordered take-out from Tia's—my favorite local Mexican restaurant. Tia's is a prototypical hole-in-the-wall run by a woman named Tia Sanchez—one of the sweetest women I have ever met. She and her family immigrated to the United States in the 1980s, her mother and father working as migrant farm laborers who eventually landed in Arkansas. Several years ago, Tia decided to open a restaurant here in Clear Springs, as her mother had passed down years of family recipes originating from Mexico. I am convinced that Tia's tamales are the world's best—especially her pork tamales with *verde* sauce. My mouth waters as I anticipate diving into one.

I fix a plate for myself and look around the room. The same people who sent me to the mountain are here to welcome me home. Trish has continued the mountain theme of my send-off party, but this time, the mountain cake has a special little flag at the very top that reads "Marren was here." I can't help but smile when I see this thoughtful gesture. Happy tears follow, and I make my way through a sea of well-wishers who ask me about my trip.

"What was it like to summit, Marren?"

"Did you get cold? Did the elevation make you sick?"

"Did you get scared?"

"Did you ever want to quit?"

As I'm happily responding to all of these questions, it occurs to me that I must look awful after the long flight home and the long drive back to Clear Springs. I haven't properly done my hair or makeup in over seventy-two hours. I wasn't expecting guests upon my return.

A quick glance at the mirror that hangs on my living room wall confirms my paranoia. Disheveled hair. Oily face. No lipstick, which my mother taught me was always necessary for a Southern lady to be presentable in public. It's official—I look pretty haggard.

I feel a sudden urge to head to my bathroom and fix myself up, but Molly sits down next to me. She hands me a CD. It is cracked and weathered and faded, having likely been neglected in some fabric case for the last twenty years.

Mariah Carey's Greatest Hits. I feel a smile start to spread across

out my closet the other day. I just want you to know that I m here you if you need me. Trish told me about Brody. I had no idea that things were so bad. I'm so sorry, Mare."

I feel like crying.

"I want our friendship back. I miss you."

"Oh, Molly, I miss you, too! I'm so sorry I didn't tell you. I just couldn't. My life was supposed to be . . . perfect."

"Oh, sweetie," she says. "Don't we all wish for perfect, and somehow never get it?"

We share a hug and promise to get back in touch, throwing out potential dates for lunch next week. Molly tells me she has to leave early, because she has to get home to her husband, Brett—also one of our high school friends—and their twins, Mary Susan and Milam. I thank her again for the CD, and she whispers, "Marren Halleck, I'm so proud of you. You are truly my hero."

Hero. Just like the Mariah Carey song we used to sing over and over again as kids. Tears fall, more hugs follow, and just like that, I seem to have my best friend back.

An hour or so later, the last of the guests head out. George and Trish lag behind with more questions. They appear so proud of me, like I am their own, and in a way, I guess I am. They seemed thrilled that Brody had married me—a "good girl"—instead of the stereotypical dumb blond. Trish had once told Brody to "date the smart, sweet girl," and this had played a role in his decision to ask me out. At least that's what Brody once told me.

"Well, Trish," George says, tugging at his short gray beard. "Guess we better let our little Marren girl get her rest. We're so proud of you, honey," George says as he comes over and gives me a loving squeeze. "Brody would be too."

I look at Trish's face, which transforms into an ashen wasteland. Grief is written in her eyes. She looks down and closes them, then looks up again as she reaches for her cup of tea.

"That reminds me," Trish says. "Tara called today. She'd like us to meet with her again next week in Little Rock. There are some things we need to discuss with respect to the lawsuit." Trish downs a sip of ginger tea—her favorite stress reliever to date, she has claimed.

I can feel my face begin to rearrange itself. My brows furrow with concern. My smile fades, and my lips tangle together in a worried web of tension. The last thing that I want to do is to go to Little Rock to see Tara. I've just spent the last two weeks trying to move forward. The lawsuit will only take me backward.

Tears well in my eyes. From the look on George's face, he knows he's made something of an emotional misstep. He quickly corrects course.

"Well, anyway, we love you, sweet girl. Way to go! What are you planning to do now?"

I shrug my shoulders, which actually represents the way I feel. Truly, I have no idea. I know I need a job, but right after Brody died, when I asked George about helping me find one, he shook his head. "Not right now," he said. "Trish and I will help you out for a while. There'll be plenty of time for that later." Since then, one particular idea has been brewing inside of me, and so I throw it out there.

"I'm gonna try to write an article for *Ladies Outdoor*," I say. "I plan to submit it soon. It's gonna be called *Five Things I Learned from Climbing Kilimanjaro*. Hopefully, they'll publish it."

This brings smiles to both George's and Trish's faces.

I lean into her warm, slender body, hugging her tight.

"Thank you. Your love means the world to me."

Chris pops into my head again. I wonder if George and Trish would still love me if they knew.

52

AFTER GEORGE AND TRISH LEAVE, I take a *real* shower—the kind you can take in the comfort of your own bathroom, lingering under hot, steaming water for as long as you want, slathering on shampoo and conditioner and body wash that doesn't come out of some tiny little tube. I suddenly feel like a brand-new person.

Decked in fresh, silky-smooth pajamas, I am me again. I dry my hair and settle into bed with *Wild*, fully prepared to finish it. I'm so close now, just a couple of chapters away. Once again, thoughts of my trip stream through my mind. So does the email to Chris. I struggle to concentrate on Cheryl Strayed's words as I grapple with a constant desire to check my phone, knowing that as long as Chris is on safari, he doesn't have the reception to answer it.

I scroll through Facebook for a while, then flip the lamp off, my eyes falling prey to jetlag. It is only 7:30 in the evening, but I can no longer hold them open. I bury my head into my pillow, hopeful that I can sleep for the entire night.

▲ ▲ ▲

I wake up at three in the morning, drenched in sweat. The room is pitch black, and the wind is howling eerily outside. My heart is pounding.

It was just a dream. *Thank God, it was only a dream.*

Actually, it was a *nightmare*. Like the ones that Brody used to have.

I was back on Kilimanjaro, climbing along the Western Breach, the route that Simon had warned was much too dangerous to take. I didn't want to do it, but Chris had begged me. "We can sleep *inside* the crater," he said. And of course, I had agreed. Anything to sleep ┕━━ ┉┉╵⊦┝ Chris.

Now, I am terrified and sweaty, ┕┉┉ ╷┕┉┉┉┉┉ ┉ ╷╷╷ only something I imagined. Still, it continues to disturb me.

Why would I have such an alarming dream?

Maybe there is something I should know about Chris. Maybe he is bad news. Maybe this dream is some kind of bellwether, warning me of danger ahead if I continue down this path of obsession over a man I barely know. I roll around in bed, tossing and turning, trying to get back to sleep, but I can't get the sight of that massive rock out of my head. Visions of the Western Breach swim around in my mind. So do visions of Chris. Finally, I feel myself becoming sleepy again, and I pray my slumber will remain nightmare free.

▲ ▲ ▲

When daylight rouses me, I am once again convinced that I'm back on the mountain. I roll over, nestling into my bed the same way that

I would nestle into my sleeping bag, burrowing for comfort, fighting the call to rise. My alarm officially blares in an old-school phone tone that forces me from slumber and into the turn-off-the-alarm position. I sit up in my bed, and I swear that I see Chris, sitting beside me, saying hello, asking me what's wrong. I try to answer him, but he cannot hear me. It's as though I am in an alternative universe, looking down on reality below. The image is so real that I'm disturbed.

Am I dreaming again?

I've read several accounts of post-climb hallucinations before, but I never actually believed them. Something about the high altitude and lack of oxygen caused many a Kilimanjaro veteran to see things that weren't real—usually soon after they summited. One woman described her experience as similar to an acid trip, like she was high on LSD. I've never taken LSD. Perhaps this is my first acid-like trip.

The image of Chris soon fades, and I'm left alone in my bed, searching for reasons to get out of it.

The silence in my room is unsettling. Once again, I long to be back on the expedition, where the beginning of days was filled with the sounds of porters and cooks and guides and climbers clamoring around together at camp, rising to feast in a tiny tent, preparing to tackle a giant objective. Here, there is mere quiet. Nothingness. A lack of anything or anyone inspiring me to do anything.

But I am a chameleon. I must change my colors to survive.

So—despite my nagging desire to pull the covers up over my head—I spring from my bed and into the shower again. Refreshed by the smell of my lavender shampoo and cocoa butter body wash, I towel off and head to the kitchen for the day's first cup of coffee.

I place a Keurig pod into the machine and press the medium-sized cup on the front. Seconds later, a steaming mug awaits its splash of my favorite hazelnut creamer. Caffeine in hand, I set up my laptop on the kitchen table, undeterred by my lack of motivation and crippling loneliness. Coffee is suddenly my new inspiration, uttering words of encouragement.

Keep going. One day at a time, Marren. It breathes a stream of white vapor from my favorite Pottery Barn mug—a gift from Trish for my twenty-fifth birthday. *Twenty-five.* The age by which I was supposed to become a published novelist. Now, I'm almost thirty, and I still haven't authored any novels.

Since I was a little girl, I've wanted to write a book. But the world ~~~~~~~~~~ be ruthless. *I can't do it. It's too much.* I want to put the

I power up my computer and begin to type. ~~~~~~~~~~ will start by attempting to write an article for *Ladies Outdoor.* I long to see the lessons I learned from Kilimanjaro staring back at me in bold, black lettering. I take another sip of coffee.

You can do this, Marren.

A new, blank Word document appears before me on the screen, ready for me to bring it to life.

"Five Things I Learned from Climbing Mount Kilimanjaro," I type.

The rest of it comes to me easily, like music to Elton John, and I bang away at the keyboard, the words melting together perfectly.

53

I TYPE FOR WHAT SEEMS LIKE HOURS, filling the screen with happy memories of my time in Africa. A first draft is officially born. I close my laptop, and I promise myself that I'll revise it later.

"The first draft of anything is shit," Ernest Hemingway once said. I couldn't agree more. It's a start, though, and that is exactly what I need in my life right now. *A new beginning. A new color.*

I refill my coffee mug, realizing that I'm fresh out of hazelnut creamer. *Damn.* I pull open a drawer, finding a packet of French vanilla Coffee mate that I snagged from a restaurant just in case. It comes to my rescue as I dump it in and watch it dissolve into an invisible new flavor.

In spite of the endless stream of caffeine I've been consuming, jetlag creeps up on me again. Though it's just after two, I feel myself getting sleepy. I decide to watch a movie, hoping that it will capture my attention enough to keep me awake. I head to the couch, where I grab the remote and flip on the TV.

My heart wants a chick flick, a tissue-worthy romance, but my head wants something deeper, more complex. I am intrigued by some of the choices that appear on my screen. Two in particular: *Wild*—which I've already seen but loved enough to watch again (plus I just finished the book!)—and *Everest,* a story about an expedition to Mount Everest that ended in absolute tragedy, based on *Into Thin Air.* Two great options between which I am torn. I end up selecting the latter, only because I haven't seen it yet.

I draw my coffee nearer, and my senses are kick-started. I hit play and am transported into the world of mountain-climbing suspense, something to which I can now relate.

begins and I am fascinated by Josh Brolin's time-

54

JETLAG FINALLY DEFEATS ME. I fall asleep during the last forty minutes of *Everest*, and when I wake, the credits are rolling. I turn off the TV, annoyed that I'll have to go back and re-watch the parts that I missed. I check the time. Seven at night. *Great.* My body has successfully mixed up its days and nights.

The daylight is fading into darkness outside, and I head to the kitchen for something to eat. I open the refrigerator to find one of Trish's signature chicken and dumpling casseroles, along with a note taped to it. *Please enjoy, you were sleeping when I snuck in to deliver it and I didn't want to wake you! We know you're probably too tired to cook or go out. Love, Trish*

Delight dances through me. What a pleasant surprise.

Trish has been doing this for years now, bringing me lovely home-cooked meals—especially in the toughest years with Brody, when she knew I lacked the mental energy to even attempt dinner. I think she felt sorry for me, like his addiction was her fault, so she tried her best to make up for something she didn't do. With each dinner delivery, guilt was etched all over her face. It lingered in the deep lines that bordered her eyes and lips. The once-bright twinkle in her eyes was gone. No matter how many dinners she brought, she couldn't fix things.

Damn you, drugs.

I remove her lovely gift from the fridge. It resides in a ceramic nine-by-thirteen-inch casserole dish, one she probably purchased at Karla's Kitchen, a local shop founded by one of Clear Springs's most talented residents, Karla McBride. Trish has a million casserole dishes from Karla's. She collects them, in fact.

Karla put Clear Springs on the national map years ago, hav-'... show competition for her incomparable cooking

here

I dump a healthy serving of casserole into a bowl into the microwave. As I wait for it to heat up, I sit at the kitchen table again and study my phone, hopeful that the few hours during which I've been asleep have somehow produced a response from Chris.

What are you doing, Marren? He's still on safari.

I touch the mail icon and jump into my inbox anyway, desperate to see something, *anything*, from him. But there is nothing. I scroll on through other messages, my disappointment slowly evolving into agony. I'm not sure why, but the idea of never talking to Chris again continues to pummel my soul. I just want *one more* chance to see him, just *one more* conversation. I can't have one more of anything with Brody. But I can somehow try again with Chris, in spite of the fact that I'm not even sure what "trying again" means. I just want to hear from him, to get some type of acknowledgment, to gain some type of closure.

The microwave beeps and I walk over to remove my dinner, eyeing it with great anticipation. Carbs have always been my go-to in times of trouble, and something about a big bowl of Trish's homemade chicken and dumpling casserole tells me that everything will be okay. I sit down at the kitchen table to scroll through my Facebook feed, and as I shove a bite of dumpling into my mouth, I see something that shocks me.

A picture. Of me—*and Chris*. Kissing at the top of Kilimanjaro. I nearly drop the fork as I study the two of us, our lips locked together at 19,341 feet, standing next to one another in colorful down jackets, me looking happier than I have in a very long time. Out Yonder has posted this and tagged me. There are also other pictures of the six of us—me, Chris, Leslie, Seri, Claire, and Casey—trekking up the mountain together, acting silly, taking in the wildlife and braving the terrain and the invisible agony of the altitude.

I scoop another bite of casserole onto my fork, and a text pops up on my phone. It's from Molly.

"I see you had an even better time than you told me you had," she wrote. "He's no Leo DiCaprio, but he sure is nice to look at. Tell me more! Btw, has Trish seen this?"

I'm sure that she is referring to the picture of the kiss. And her classic "Tell me more" is a line that she coined years ago, one we used jokingly when gossip sprung up from unexpected places.

Like the time when Katie Billings supposedly slept with Brian Yates, and his parents caught them red-handed in their master bedroom. Or the time when Kristin Kaufman made copies of Tate Landry's note to Lydia Mason (the girl he was sleeping with on the side) and distributed them all over school. *No way. Tell me more.*

Or when Kara Stevens's dad left her mom for Sam McClure's mom.

Whaaat? Tell me more.

Back then, it was fun. But now, the gossip is at my own expense. I don't want to *tell her more*, and so I don't. Though I long to reconnect with Molly, I cannot pretend that we are kids again. I cannot share my feelings about Chris. We're adults now, and things are much too complicated to reduce to small-town gossip, the way we used to.

I feel myself blushing. What happened in this picture is no one's business. This is private, something between Chris and me only. It has nothing to do with Molly. Or Trish for that matter. I decide not to answer Molly's text.

55

I OPEN MY LAPTOP and begin to tinker with the article that I'm attempting to write for *Ladies Outdoor*. Before I know it, I've been playing around with words on a computer screen for the better part of three hours. Thankfully, the night is getting older, and the chance that I will sleep through it is increasing with each hour that I remain awake.

Molly has scolded me nicely for not texting her back, yet I don't care. My mind can't seem to veer from Chris and the kiss picture, or the possibility that he may never return my email message.

As I sit at the kitchen table, staring at my computer screen, a sweet memory of Brody crosses my mind. Three years ago, I was up late writing, as I generally was, in this very same spot. He startled me at one in the morning, claiming to be unable to sleep. I remember the way he walked slowly and silently toward me, gently wrapping his arms around my stiff, dedicated neck when he finally reached me. His strong biceps had always incited a feeling of security within me, but on that particular night, they conjured something more. He squeezed tighter, and I squeezed back. The tension grew between us, and I felt compelled to stand up and follow him to our bedroom. I still remember the words he said to me that night, after we made love.

"I'll never love anyone the way I love you, Marren Halleck," he said. It was one of the few nights that he seemed to possess some clarity, the kind he used to have before the hydrocodone. Part of me wondered if he'd actually *tried* to quit that night—a genuine, gut-wrenching attempt to forgo his nightly dose of death from those tiny, circular pills. Perhaps that's why he couldn't sleep. Perhaps that's why he wanted to be with me for the first time in so long that I ~~couldn't~~ even remember when the last time was. The drugs had

~~wished I let him~~

more. *Unseen. Unheard.*

Maybe I don't want the crappy circumstances of my life to go without notice.

Maybe I want to *matter* to someone again.

▲ ▲ ▲

I manage to read about fifty pages before falling asleep, book in hand. A loud thud wakes me briefly around midnight, and I'm relieved to find that it's only the sound of my book crashing to the floor. I fall into a deep slumber again, and I don't wake until 4:30 a.m. Though it's way too early, in the world of jetlag, sleeping until 4:30 a.m. is a small victory.

Though I'm awake now, the darkness inhibits my desire to get out of bed. I grab my phone from the nightstand beside me and instinctively check Facebook and email for any sign of Chris. The pessimistic voice in my head is still discouraging me, reminding me that I will likely strike dirt instead of gold.

What are you thinking? He's never going to respond. You'll never talk to Chris—or Brody, for that matter—again.

Shut up, nasty voice. I want to take it down like a sniper, to strike it dead once and for all. But I can't. To my chagrin, the nasty foe-voice might just be right. I put the phone back down on the nightstand and throw my hands over my face. I want to cry but the tears won't come.

Then, a ping. A middle-of-the-night text.

From Chris. *Please be from Chris.*

But it's from Molly. What is she doing up so early? Or is this actually late?

"All right," she wrote, "I've been into the wine. And I'm telling you, if you don't spill the beans, I'm going to track this guy down and ask him myself!"

Been into the wine? Of course she has. Molly has never been shy about drinking too much. But usually she's a "social drinker." At least that's what she liked to call it. Apparently, her "social drinking" has taken a turn for the worse. Texts at 4:30 a.m. are never a good match with alcohol.

I'm going to have to answer her. Otherwise, her "social drinking" might drive her to do something crazier than a 4:30 a.m. text.

"He was just a friend I met on the trip. Thought it would be funny to kiss me at the top. It was all a big joke. Nothing to tell. I haven't talked to him since I left Tanzania." The last sentence of my text is true, but I hope the rest of it is not.

If I know Molly, this won't be enough to quell her curiosity. Still, it's the best I've got right now. It's my story and I'm sticking to it. I send the text, and she doesn't respond. Maybe her "social drinking" has finally driven her to sleep.

I'm still in bed, wondering what I'm going to do at this hour. So I play around on my phone, surfing the world of social media.

Facebook. Instagram. Twitter. In that order. Too many braggarts, too many filters, too many people who think they are more important than I am. That they know best. I cannot handle it anymore.

I click over to my email, and my heart swells with joy. Staring back at me from my inbox is an email from Leslie, asking me how I'm doing and inviting me to visit her home with Seri in New Orleans next month for what sounds like a Kilimanjaro reunion. Chris is included in the email chain, as are Casey and Claire. The invitation gives me new life, a new reason to keep working on the ~~Outdoor~~ and a new hope to believe that my I'll-

56

THE LAST WEEK has wreaked a new kind of havoc on me. I *still* haven't heard from Chris, and it's slowly killing me.

I think of my writer friend Eliza—who wrote a novel and queried some agents—and how she once told me that the hardest part of her journey to land an agent wasn't writing the book itself, but the waiting to hear back. Sometimes, the agents would respond within a week or two, Eliza said. Others took up to six or eight months. I can imagine Eliza checking her inbox every single day for six to eight months, waiting for someone she didn't know to accept or reject the words that she worked so hard to put on over three hundred pages.

Now, I can finally relate to Eliza. I am sitting around, checking my own inbox every day, waiting for a man I hardly know to accept or reject words that my heart worked so hard to say. The waiting is the hardest part.

And today, I am waiting for an altogether different reason. This time, I am sitting in the lobby of a law firm, about to meet with Tara. Trish and George are beside me. I guess I should be glad they decided to do this, because the lawsuit—along with my upcoming trip to New Orleans—are the only things keeping my mind off Chris now.

Tara walks in, looking more radiant than the first time we met. Her tailored pantsuit is a flattering shade of red, and her peep-toe black patent heels show off matching red toenail polish. She is wearing a simple gold necklace that ties the outfit together like a neat bow.

"Good afternoon, Halleck Family," she says. Her expression is sincere, but not as warm as I hoped. Something about it turns my stomach into a mangled mess.

She takes a seat across from us and removes some papers from ̶ ̶ ̶ "I ̶ ̶ ̶ subpoena for Marren to be deposed next

I nod.

"Between now and then, that's exactly what I'm gonna do. Ensure that you are as prepared as possible for this deposition."

I nod again. I feel like a kid on the diving board, being cheered on by pushy peers. They are screaming that I can do it, that I should just close my eyes and jump in. Some of them tell me to count to ten before I jump. Others tell me not to look. So many people telling me how to do something I'm not yet ready for. And yet I heed their advice, and finally, I take the leap.

In no time at all, I'll be leaping into this deposition, with Tara cheering me on.

▲ ▲ ▲

After the meeting with Tara, I exchange emails with Leslie, trying to nail down all the details of my trip to New Orleans for our

Kilimanjaro reunion. It sounds like so much fun. I am still too terrified to ask her whether Chris plans to be there too.

I study the back of Trish's head as George drives to Loca Luna—one of our favorite dinner spots in Little Rock. Trish's hair is thinner now, graying in places that it never had before. I wonder if I am contributing to this. Just a few days ago, we had a massive fallout over the Facebook picture of Chris kissing me at the summit of Kilimanjaro. After the picture was posted, judgment ensued. And the judgers—many of whom were Clear Springs residents that I'd never actually met—apparently berated George and Trish. For this, I paid the price.

The morning after the photo surfaced, Trish phoned and asked me to come over. She told me there was something we needed to discuss. I assumed she meant the picture, and I wondered what she intended to say. The troubled look on her face when she opened her bright red front door told me that our conversation wouldn't end well.

Trish—the sweet, proper, generous Southern lady—actually accused me of taking her and George's money just so I could go over to another country and "screw" a stranger in an exotic location to cope. Appalled by her words, I had no response. *Grief is a troubling, transformative thing.*

As bad as things had gotten with Trish, things with Molly got even worse.

A couple of days after I arrived home, Molly came over with a bottle of wine, in what I believed was an attempt to try and rekindle our friendship. Though it was a tiny bit awkward, it felt good to have someone to talk to. She settled in Brody's old chair, seemingly ready to lend a listening ear. Something about it felt familiar and safe. We *had* been best friends for most of our lives. I hadn't had a "girls' night" in as long as I could remember. The pills had worn many hats in this household, including that of a warden. Escaping to normal life seemed almost impossible.

Molly poured wine for each of us. She told me about her husband, Brett—whom I've also known since I was a kid, someone I've never been particularly fond of—and ranted on about the way he never helps her with the kids and the fact that she might actually go insane without her nightly dose of wine. Before I knew it, we moved on to a second bottle, an extra Cabernet that I had received as a gift from a neighbor to celebrate my Kilimanjaro trip.

_____d bottle of wine that forced the words out of

our nights in the tent on the mountain, the way _ _ secrets, the way I'd blown up when he left, the way he still hadn't responded to the email that I didn't mean to send. I even showed her the email, which I pulled up from my "sent" items. Molly's eyes had widened. It was as if she'd struck oil in the gossip field. She left my house after midnight, and I was amazed that the jetlag hadn't caused me to pass out.

The next day, I woke up in a fog. My head was pounding. I struggled to remember that Molly and I had conversed over two bottles of wine, and I couldn't recall exactly what I'd said. Oh, no. What had I told her?

My headache worsened, and I realized that I was out of ibuprofen, so I drove to Gus's Market, the local convenience store, which is located right next to The Calico Café, our local coffee shop. Just as I was about to enter Gus's, Colette McSwain came out of the café, holding a takeout cup of coffee. When she saw me, she gave me the up-and-down eye assessment.

"Hey, Marren," Colette said, her blond hair pulled back into a tight bun. "How's your new man? Did y'all meet on *Traveling Singles* dot com?" She laughed out loud. "Molly texted me last night—guess you two had a little late-night chat? Absolutely unbelievable. Brody hasn't even been dead a year, and you're chasing some new guy halfway across the world."

I was tempted to fight back, to defend my honor, but nothing I could have said would have changed her scathing small-town opinion. I walked into Gus's and bought some ibuprofen, thinking that I just might take the whole bottle.

Now, we're about to walk into Loca Luna after our meeting with Tara, and though I know I shouldn't, I somehow wish I could consume a whole bottle of wine.

57

know now

have both fought so hard to come to terms with this.

On the very same day that *Ladies Outdoor* offered to publish my article, Trish showed up at my front door with a casserole in hand. I opened the door, and a lingering silence between us signified the fact that we hadn't spoken for three whole days. She was dressed to the nines, wearing a tailored, kelly-green dress and pearls, like she was about to attend some fancy country club luncheon.

Approximately ten seconds passed, and she opened her mouth.

"I'm sorry, Marren," she said, offering the casserole to me with both hands. "It's just that I miss him so much. And I know how much he loved you, even if he didn't always act like it. It's hard for me to see you moving on so fast."

I accepted the casserole from her and took a long, slow, deep breath, just before I invited her in. We moved to the kitchen, where I placed the casserole in the freezer and then turned to face her as she found a seat on the barstool of the kitchen island.

"Thanks for this," I finally managed.

"Marren, I hope you're okay," she said. She hesitated, like she wanted to ask me something, and then she just spit her thoughts right out. "Are you still seeing this man in the Kilimanjaro picture?"

As much as I'd have loved to say yes, I couldn't.

"No," I said. "And actually, I never was *seeing him*."

"But what about the kiss?"

"It just kind of . . . happened. You have no idea what it's like up there, Trish. The lack of oxygen can make you crazy. We were just two determined human beings, each coping with our own kind of loss, our own kind of resilience, losing ourselves in a moment that most people will never experience. The kiss meant nothing."

I tried to believe myself as I spoke the words, but I couldn't.

Thankfully, Trish did.

"I haven't even talked to him since we left Africa," I said.

"Oh, sweet Marren," she said, coming over to hug me. "I hope you'll forgive me. I just thought . . . I don't even know what I thought. We all just . . . We're having a hard time coping with everything. And now I see that you are too."

"Thanks for understanding," I said, trying my best to gather some composure. "Some good news is that *Ladies Outdoor* has agreed to publish my article."

"Your article?"

"Yes. I wrote a piece on the climb. *Five Things I Learned from Climbing Mount Kilimanjaro.*"

"Wow! When can we read it?"

"It'll come out in a few months. I'll be sure that you get a copy. I can't ever thank you enough for sending me over to that mountain. You have no idea what I learned. How much I've grown. The people that I met." As I said the last of these words, I suddenly wondered if she would read anything into them.

Trish smiled, then looked down at the ground. When she finally looked up, I saw that her dark blue eyes had faded into a beautiful turquoise color, ripe with tears.

"I know what he did to you, Marren," she said. "I know how much Brody hurt you. For that, I can never apologize enough. The truth is that we just want you to be okay. I know that our son would want you to be okay. I prayed every day that he would finally break through to the other side, to lean on his family and not on the pills, but my prayers didn't work. I never understood why."

͏ ͏ ͏ Trish's left cheek, following a linear

know that you ͏ ͏
being a daughter to us."

She hugged me tightly and I felt better, reminded of the way my own mother used to hug me before the accident. I fell into her arms and began to bawl, unable to fight back the years of emotion that came bursting out of me like raging water from a broken dam.

Now, I beam as our waiter emerges from nothingness, and George orders my favorite appetizer—Loca Luna's signature white cheese dip.

"Just for you, sweetie," he says, like a doting father. "I know how much you love it."

▲ ▲ ▲

Two weeks later, I'm back in Little Rock. Tara is more casual today. It's a Saturday, and the office is closed. It's just us. I think she probably planned it this way. To make things more weekend-like, to take some of the business-week pressure away.

She has explained the kind of things I should expect to hear at my deposition. She has also explained the things I need to say and do, along with things I shouldn't say or do. And then she suggests that we practice.

I nod. *I can do this.* Tara's presence is calming. I like how she speaks to me in a soothing tone, like I am a child, and she is patting my back, telling me that it's all going to be okay.

As long as Tara is here, I will survive this.

"Let's try a few questions," she says, pacing back and forth in front of me. "Mrs. Halleck, when did you first learn that your husband had a problem with drugs?"

I tense up. I don't really know. Maybe I should have. Maybe if I'd figured it out sooner, he would still be here. Guilt chases me now in a game of hide-and-seek. I'm hiding. Guilt is seeking.

I close my eyes. "I, um, I'm not sure. I guess—"

"You're not sure?" Tara repeats, her tone harsh now, like nails on a chalkboard.

"I guess it was about six months after the injury."

"Six months? So you are saying that it took you six months to realize he had a problem? You didn't try to intervene sooner, before the addiction turned deadly?"

I shudder at Tara's mock question. This isn't my fault. Except now I feel like it is.

"Mrs. Halleck, please, answer the question."

"I didn't know," I say, my voice raised. "He got injured, and then they gave him the pills and he started acting strange. I wasn't sure what was going on. All I knew was that he started taking more and more pills—"

"Stop," Tara says. "Remember to only answer the question you are asked. Don't give them any more information than they are requesting. And if you get frazzled, it's always okay to take a breather by asking them to rephrase the question."

I take a deep breath. This is harder than I thought it would be.

"Let's try this again. Mrs. Halleck, is it true that you didn't try to help Brody for six months?"

I stare at Tara, knowing that she is deliberately trying to shake me.

"Can you please rephrase the question?"

"Sure. Is it true that you did nothing to intervene in your hus-

done for six months after it began?"

ter about everything

58

THE DAY HAS FINALLY COME. I am set to leave for New Orleans to reunite with my Kilimanjaro climbing crew. My heart flutters with anticipation, and yet at the same time, it's heavy with regret—because I still haven't heard from Chris. And every single time that my fingers find the courage to pull up his cell number or his email address, something in my brain slaps them away.

Don't do this, Marren. If he really wants to talk to you, he'll call you. He'll email you.

I load the car and start it up, plugging in my iPhone and selecting my new playlist, "Kili Reunion." I turn up "Someday" by Rob Thomas, remembering the feeling of hope it created within me on my flight to Africa. I hold on to hope that someday, I will see Chris again. And maybe that someday will be this weekend. When I dared to question Leslie about whether Chris planned to attend, her answer was a soft "maybe."

My 2015 Toyota Camry—a gift from Brody in the good times—hums along a desolate stretch of I-55, the tires spinning enthusiastically along the pavement at somewhere around seventy-five miles per hour. My mind is focused on seeing New Orleans for the first time, and I'm suddenly puzzled by the fact that, being from Arkansas, Brody and I never ventured down to such a popular location. I've seen pictures and heard stories of Mardi Gras, particularly from one of Brody's baseball teammates, Jeremy— who played with Brody at the University of Arkansas—but I've never experienced any of it in person. We once went to dinner with Jeremy and his then-girlfriend, Samantha, and, tipsy on Knob Creek whiskey, Jeremy shared endless stories of his own personal Mardi Gras experiences—crowds and beads and masks and floats ᵃ ᵇ ᵃᵗˢ all doused in a sea of purple and yellow and

too complex to be entirely comprehended, throwing beads on end. According to Jeremy, these outfits—long, heavy beaded bodices and sprawling, peacock-like feather attachments measuring up to ten feet in diameter—were so elaborate that the women had to wear adult diapers, for a trip to relieve their bladders during the parade madness was completely out of the question. The things some people might consider shocking were actually quite normal in New Orleans, Jeremy said.

I turn up Toto's "Africa" when it comes on, wondering what kind of shocking new normal lies ahead for me on this Kilimanjaro reunion weekend in The Big Easy.

▲ ▲ ▲

The house on Carondelet Street is even more fantastic than I imagined. Because they are doctors, I just assumed that Seri and Leslie would share an impressive abode, but this far exceeds my expectations. Nestled inside New Orleans's famous Garden District, the façade of the house is marked by columns and a front porch/balcony combo to die for.

I ring the doorbell, and a smiling Leslie opens the front door, which is defined by a lovely combination of wood and glass panes. She offers me a big hug, and I accept, awed by the grandiosity of their home.

As I enter, an antique French chandelier dangles above me, its dainty curvature accentuated with its chateau-like candelabra bulbs. The weathered wooden floor of the foyer is almost entirely masked by an exquisite area rug, situated underneath a French-country pedestal table—in the center of which sits an arrangement of fresh white hydrangea, which reminds of my mother. I already feel at home.

Seri meets me in the foyer as I admire the flowers.

"Marren!" she says, with great enthusiasm. "We are so happy to see you. Please, join us in the living room."

I follow her into an open room that merges with the kitchen. My eyes are immediately drawn to the fireplace, which features a uniquely carved mantel that appears to be made of marble, along with an arched, cast iron insert that screams of a hundred-plus-year history. Two love seat settees flank each side of the room, and one large, tufted sofa runs masterfully perpendicular to them. On one of the settees, I see the familiar faces of Casey and Claire, and I run over to hug both.

"Casey! Claire! I'm so glad to see you. Where are your T-shirts?"

Everyone laughs.

"We left them at home," Claire says.

There is laughter among us, followed by an awkward silence. I dare to ask the question that's been burning in my mind for weeks now.

"Is Chris here?" I say.

"He's on his way," Seri announces as Leslie delivers two neatly crafted cocktails to Casey and Claire.

My heart quickens. The feeling that comes over me reminds me of the time when I was standing beside my locker in high school, shoving a chemistry textbook inside as I removed an English text-book, worn with yellowed pages, preparing to brave Mrs. Gardner and her literary prowess when Brody appeared behind me. Our relationship was brand new, born into exclusivity after only two
~~idea where~~ it would lead.

wanted to run free, shout out, tell the world that I was going with Brody Halleck, Clear Springs's star baseball hero. This was sure to make me famous. Even in pre–social media times, I knew that the news would get around in Clear Springs faster than one of Brody's pitches.

Of course I said yes. And my heart, racing with sheer excitement and anticipation, beat faster on that day than perhaps any other in my life.

Now, my heart is working hard once again, trying not to leap from my chest. *Chris is on his way.* The words scroll through my head, temporarily set on replay. Just like the day that Brody asked me to prom, I want to scream out, to show the world how excited I am, and yet I know that I must remain composed.

"Would you like something to drink, Marren?" Leslie asks. I've missed that sweet voice that so often comforted me on the mountain. I am very happy to hear it again.

"A glass of wine would be perfect," I say.

"Red or white?"

"Red, if you have it."

"*If* we have it," Seri says with a sly smile. She nods to a hallway and leads me—along with our entire crew—to another room. We walk through an arched doorway to a large, open space enclosed in brick, glass, and wood. It is the most impressive wine cellar I've ever seen. There appear to be hundreds of bottles of wine that live here.

"Do you have a favorite kind of red?" Seri says, very pensively. "Because chances are that if you do, we have it here for you. We're something of wine connoisseurs. We went to Napa Valley on our honeymoon."

A smile expands across my face as I shrug my shoulders.

"I'm just a girl from Clear Springs, Arkansas," I say. "I'm used to cheap red wine in a Solo cup. I'll take whatever you're willing to give me. Believe me, I'm not picky."

The group erupts in laughter, and I am reminded of our meals together on Kilimanjaro. There was always a lot of laughter in the dining tent. It's good to be back with Seri and Leslie and Casey and Claire, and it will be good to see Chris. My heart flutters again as I think of him.

59

"Yes," she said. "Wish I could say that it's got a g-- ,"
She laughed a little. I liked to see Seri like this. Making a little joke,
not so serious. More than likely, she'd had some cabernet tonight too.

The smoky vanilla flavor of the wine slides gently down my
throat, enhancing my experience as we go from room to room. The
house oozes history, and I can't help but wonder about all of its fireplaces. There's one in practically every room. When I ask Seri about
them, she smiles and turns to Leslie, who happily takes the opportunity to answer.

"I'm not sure if I told you, but I'm a native New Orleans girl,"
Leslie says. "My family has been here for generations, and this
house has been in my family for over one hundred and thirty years.
Back then, they put fireplaces in most rooms for heat. There was no
central heat and air."

"Oh," I say, nodding as she continues.

"Look over there," Leslie says, pointing to a fireplace that sits in the middle of the study. In front of it is a small, elaborate screen-like piece of furniture. Leslie explains that this is an antique Victorian fireplace screen, passed down from her great-great-grandmother. Her great-great-grandfather carved the rosewood frame and legs, Leslie says, and her great-great-grandmother embroidered the floral tapestry piece that serves as the screen. I am impressed by the hues of light pink, sage, and baby blue wrapped in darker coral and cobalt and hints of pitch black. It is like staring at a picture of an antique floral arrangement, something that might have been delivered to your door circa 1870. It was used as a decorative cover to your fireplace when no fire was burning, Leslie explains. Her eyes exude pride as she says the words.

I ponder what she just said. *A decorative cover to disguise your fireplace when no fire was burning.*

That is me. Here. Right now. Smiling and pretending that everything in my life is great when no fire is burning in my soul. Brody's gone. Kilimanjaro is behind me. And Chris never responded.

But he's coming. Tonight.

Maybe there's a chance that he'll start a fire in me soon.

60

and he's supposed to meet us at the restaurant now. ~~ ↲
swirls in my stomach while I secretly practice what I might say to
him after all of this time. Honestly, I'm not sure how to react. So I
envision some different possibilities.

I can take the cool approach: "Chris! It's so good to see you
again. I've missed you. How've you been?" Or perhaps the passive-
aggressive approach: "Chris! I'm so happy you're here! Tell me,
what have you been doing these days?" (While secretly wanting to
punch him in the face and tell him how much I hate him for not
responding to my "accidental" email.) Finally, the direct approach:
"Chris. Wow. It's been a while. Care to tell me why the hell I never
heard from you after we left Kilimanjaro?"

The latter seems a bit harsh. Still, it is my first choice. I have no
idea what I'll actually say until I see him.

The limo—a black stretch Cadillac—pulls up in front of the
house, and we pile in. Buzzed on my pre-dinner wine, I revel in

the discussion of what everyone has been doing since the trip. The honeymooners describe their adjustment to marital life—Casey's expectation that only Claire would do laundry, Claire's obsession with cats and the fact that Casey doesn't want one, and their nightly spats over which Netflix series to watch next. Seri and Leslie share snippets from their experiences as physicians in New Orleans and hints of their desire to have a child together someday soon. Their descriptions are safe and superficial.

As the alcohol flows, the stories break open, beginning to bleed reality.

Claire launches into the tale of her harrowing battle with high-altitude pulmonary edema, telling us how terrified she actually was as they carried her down the mountain. Casey offers his perspective, revealing his anguish over the real possibility that Claire could die and that he would forever feel responsible, for it was he that convinced her to let go of her fear and climb the mountain with him.

When we arrive at Galatoire's, we file out of the limo, introduced to the sound of loud, drunken crowds who are aimlessly navigating their way through the French Quarter. Once inside, Claire babbles on about her time in the hospital in Arusha and how the third-world medical care made her fear for her life. Casey strokes her long blond hair and plants a gentle kiss on the top of her head as we take our seats at a nice round table for six in the back of the restaurant.

Just before the waiter approaches, I say what I believe everyone else must be thinking.

"Where is Chris? Is he really coming?"

Seri glances at her phone and shakes her head. "I have no idea. He said he'd be here." She pauses, seeming to contemplate exactly what she'll say next. "Haven't *you* talked to him, Marren? From the picture that Simon posted, the one at the summit, I figured *you'd* have a much better idea of whether he's coming than I do." Her tone is so sharp and direct that it troubles me, despite my familiarity with her strong personality.

Before I can take offense to Seri's words, Leslie chimes in, tempering the caustic lull that now lingers around the table. "What she means is . . . do tell us, Marren! Is there something going on between the two of you? And if there is, why are you keeping it so quiet?"

It's the most pressing thing I've ever heard escape from Leslie's mouth. Normally, she is cautious and diplomatic—definitely not one to pry.

[. . .] answer our lanky, brown-haired, college-aged waiter [. . .]

back at me too. I am cornered.

"It's a long story," I say.

"We've got nothing but time," says Claire, her voice laced with quick wit.

I take a sip of my drink and proceed to answer. "If you really must know, Chris and I haven't talked since we left Tanzania. The last time we spoke was at the hotel the night before he left for safari. I was scheduled to fly out the next day."

All four sets of eyes are focused on me now, each person at the table waiting for what I am going to say next—I feel like I am performing on stage in front of a crowd of hungry critics.

"Anyway, there's nothing to tell. The kiss on the mountain was no more than an adrenaline rush for him. That's it. He told me he didn't want to pursue it any further. It was just too complicated."

My tiny audience suddenly looks deflated, like the episode of the TV show they were watching didn't end as they'd expected.

"But he seemed so into you," says Claire.

I tilt my head, curious about her comment. Had Chris, in fact, been *into* me? "If that was the case," I say, feeling emboldened, "why haven't we spoken since Africa? Why isn't he here now?"

Everyone looks down, and Claire fiddles with her napkin set. It is Seri who sets the tone again, ensuring that it will remain serious and not sad.

"He said that he's coming," she says, her voice commanding our attention. "And I'm sure that he will."

61

our group. "Not to boast," she says, her smile

I've visited more famous restaurants in New Orleans than anyone I know, and I possess the superpower of knowing exactly what to order at each of them."

Leslie nods, adding, "Of the two of us, Seri's the true foodie."

Claire seems especially impressed.

"How did you eat any of that stuff on our Kilimanjaro trip?" Claire says, her eyes squinted as they wait for Seri's answer.

"It wasn't easy. On the mountain, the food was mediocre at best. Although, I found the food in Arusha to be spectacular. Still, I would dream of shrimp remoulade almost every night."

We all laugh and then launch into more stories of life on Kilimanjaro—of the wonderful things that we saw and experienced. Simon's Swahili lessons. The beauty of the rainforest. The way the porters would gather and sing nightly.

When I mention Uhuru and my tumble down the scree, the faces around me go blank. I realize that none of the people surrounding me actually summited the mountain, due to circumstances beyond their control. Now, more than ever, I long for Chris. If he was here, he could relate.

"Well," says Seri. "Now seems like a perfect time to tell you that Leslie and I are going back. Just booked another excursion last week." She looks at Leslie and smiles. "This time, we're going all the way to Uhuru."

"We want our own kiss picture," Leslie says, looking at me.

More group laughter.

I blush, feeling honored to be here, sitting among strong, brilliant, determined people who don't quit. I will never understand why I was one of only two from our crew to make it to the top, why the mountain was so incredibly unfair.

Damn you, Chris. You still aren't here. Why?

Time presses on, and, though I know I shouldn't be drinking this much, the alcohol makes it easier to tolerate the idea that Chris is never going to show up. At almost eleven o'clock, inebriation breeds more poignant stories of our post-Kilimanjaro lives, and some of the tales being told are much too delicate to be heard.

Casey and Claire admit to a struggle with possible infertility—a disappointing result of Claire's long-term endometriosis. The baby they hoped for may never come, and this has put a strain on their relationship—a marriage so new that it lacks the bandwidth to tolerate such hardship.

Seri and Leslie confess to constantly bickering, due to perceived failure. The wind on the mountain forced them into an impossible choice, into changes of schedules for the sake of family. Seri has been particularly plagued by this goal she didn't meet, which Leslie now says has made her even harder to get along with than ever before. She's become obsessed with going back to Kilimanjaro, and her perfectionism has worsened. They, too, are struggling.

This caliber of conversation brings me to a sobering new realization. These people, with whom I spent quality time on one of the world's best-known mountains, are actually *real, regular* human beings with actual problems. Problems that they likely came to the mountain to escape. Just like me. This is both sad and reassuring at the same time. I am not the only one with problems.

Gabe continues to plunk down powerful drinks in front of me. I ˙ ˙ ˔˗˖ᵗ the strong taste of vodka, and he simply says, "This ˑ ˷ᵣₛ later. I—

"KILL-a-MAN-jaro!"

Silly, drunken laughter follows. I try to suppress a thought of Chris and his corny jokes by doing some people watching as we wait for the limo. To my left stands a naked woman whose body is covered in full body paint. To my right, a couple French kissing. Straight ahead, college kids smoking what smells like pot. Up above, a sky full of beautiful stars.

"Welcome to New Orleans!" Seri calls out into the thick night air. The drinks have torn down a wall—she apparently has a wild side. It's fun to watch, just like the people all around us.

We pile into the limo again, and Seri hands out some post-dinner beer. She suddenly starts to chant, just like the porters on the mountain. The words come together like a song, as we sing them in unison:

"Pole, pole! Pole, pole!"

Simon's words. *Slowly, slowly. Slowly, slowly.*

I raise my beer into the air, smiling vigorously. Slowly, we pull into their driveway. Slowly, we are all adjusting to life off the mountain, and tonight we have celebrated our journeys.

Taking a long, last drink, I follow the others into the house and find my room, which has been generously decorated for my short stay, complete with a tiny piece of foil-wrapped chocolate on my pillow.

"Good night, Marren!" I hear Seri say as I close the door behind me.

"Goodnight," I say. And then I fall into the bed, which has been beautifully turned down by someone I'm guessing is a live-in housekeeper, someone who must reside in the impressive guest quarters adjacent to the house. "And thank you."

Three words resound in my head when I close my eyes, just before I pass out.

He's not coming.

▲ ▲ ▲

I wake the next morning to the sound of voices downstairs and the same smell of bacon and eggs that I remember from the mountain. I get up and get dressed and I join the group for breakfast, blessed to have a warm meal instead of a semi-cold one that requires multiple layers of clothing to enjoy. I can't help but stare at Leslie as she commands the kitchen, decked in a monogrammed apron. I am reminded of my grandmother and the breakfasts we shared, and also of my mother and the meals she once prepared.

Seri looks at Leslie proudly. The same great-great-grandmother who fabulously created the antique Victorian fireplace screen apparently passed down a family tradition of talent in the kitchen. As Leslie flips a spatula over, effectively corralling the eggs, she explains that the women in her family were gifted chefs, often producing new dishes that are now notable in some of the most famous of New

Orleans restaurants. Her great-great-grandmother's gift of preparing jambalaya is rumored to have inspired a special recipe in a Louisiana cookbook back in the 1890s, she says. I picture a woman standing over a stove, wearing a ruffled apron over her demure long-sleeved blouse and full-length skirt, right here in this very kitchen. Generations of talented women have cooked here. This house is special, for many reasons.

Constant bickering or not, the couple exudes connection. Seri the selective foodie has seemingly found her perfect match in Leslie ... physician-cook.

... I am unex-

"There was a work emergency last night... route, via his family's private plane, when he had to turn around suddenly."

He's definitely not coming.

I can feel Seri's eyes on me. And everyone else's.

"What?" I say.

"Marren, are you all right?" Seri asks.

"I'm fine," I say.

No one says anything. They know I'm lying.

"What's that Swahili saying that Simon taught us? Something about the journey going on?" I ask.

"*Safari lazima iendelee,*" Seri reminds us. "The journey must continue."

"Yeah, that one," I say. "I'm *fine. Safari lazima iendelee.*"

62

AFTER A RELAXING SECOND NIGHT at the house on Carondelet Street, I am ready for the journey back to Clear Springs. We say our goodbyes, and Leslie sends us home with sugar cookies wrapped in cellophane, the landscape of Mount Kilimanjaro piped on top in fondant icing.

"I didn't make them, but I wish I had. I'm terrible at piping." I laugh as I thank her again for everything. Sweet Leslie, so much sweeter than the cookie she just handed me.

Rejuvenated by our reunion, I drive up I-55, knowing that whatever lies ahead of me I will be able to take on.

I think of how Seri was as I left this morning, her strong, commanding voice wishing me well along the way.

"You're an inspiration, Marren. Keep going," Seri said as she waved goodbye.

I'm an inspiration? To a badass female surgeon whom anyone would surely idolize? I'm beyond flattered. And I will "keep going," just as Seri has instructed, though I have absolutely no idea where I'm headed. But I know that wherever it is, I can do it on my own. I should just forget about Chris. I don't need him—or anyone else—to get to where I'm going. At least that's what I have to tell myself for now.

I stop for gas somewhere in small-town Mississippi. The little mom-and-pop store is housed in a shack along a busy stretch of road. The cars whiz by. Old ones. New ones. Big ones. Tiny ones. Eighteen-wheelers. All different ways to travel on the same stretch of road. My first ride was with Brody. Now, it's just me. *The new me*. The me that just summited one of the world's tallest mountains.

Courage warms my soul as I think of what I've done. Of what I ~~do now~~ The new me must find a different way to travel the ~~~~ I place the gas

63

IT'S DEPOSITION DAY, two weeks later, and George is wait-ing for me outside. I can hear the car running as I pick up a wedding photo of Brody and me, studying it carefully.

In the photo, we are staring lovingly at each other. I remem-ber being so nervous that day. So terrified that something would go wrong—that the most perfect day of my life would be ruined by a simple misstep that resulted in a tumble, a forgotten vow, or a cranky ring that refused to slide onto my left ring finger.

Now, imperfection has already moved in, a permanent resident in my heart. I'm afraid it might never move away.

I talk to the picture, telling Brody that I'm going to be okay. I'm going to do this for him, to fight back against that nasty thing that came into our lives and clawed its way through the depths of our marital bond.

George honks and I hurry outside.

I open the rear passenger door and slide into the seat behind Trish.

"You ready?" she asks.

I nod, because whether I am or not is irrelevant.

When we arrive, the receptionist greets us warmly at the front desk. "You all can just wait here until Mrs. Halleck is done," she says, smiling and pointing to the nicely furnished waiting room, which is full of yellow daisies and lilies and oversized chairs. It whispers warmth and loveliness, and yet I know what I'm about to do will be like opening the door to a messy, wintry blizzard, the questions about my past assaulting me like a bitterly cold storm. George and Trish hug me and wish me luck, telling me that it's all going to be okay. They have come with me to lend moral support.

"I love you Marren," George says, and for a split second I can

serves as the dark cherry conference table.

mini-Snickers, hoping that the combination of chocolate, peanuts, and caramel will somehow quell my nerves, but then I put it back, remembering that my new motto is to try and pursue people and things that help me, not hurt me.

Tara soon walks through the conference room door. Today, she is wearing a simple black pantsuit with a green blouse. It accentuates her eyes. She looks sharp and ready. I hope I am ready too.

Tara reviews the file, concentrating on a document that I cannot see. Something on the single page at which she is staring has clearly captured her attention. I wonder what it is, but I am too nervous to ask.

Around ten minutes later, the door cracks open. A young, dark-haired man with piercing blue eyes walks in and introduces himself. He is accompanied by a large, brown-haired, older-looking woman who is carrying something that looks like a laptop.

"Hello," he says. "You must be Marren?"

I nod, smiling.

"I'm Sam Clyburn. I'll be handling your deposition today. Oh, and this is Kayla. She'll be our stenographer."

I nod and smile at Sam and Kayla, who both seem nice enough. I can't help but wonder why Tara has painted opposing counsel out to be so ruthless. What am I missing?

"Well, then. Let's get started, shall we?"

▲ ▲ ▲

Thirty minutes later, I have relived some of the worst parts of Brody's addiction. I have faced questions about how it began and ended. I have even faced questions about my potential role and fault in the matter. I have answered questions about the most intimate details in my marriage. I am just about to self-implode, so I ask for a bathroom break.

Sam agrees, and I practically run out of the room, headed for the nearest women's restroom, which Tara has told me where to find. I push open the heavy wooden door and fight back tears as I find the mirror.

"How did you end up here? It wasn't supposed to be like this," I say out loud, staring at my reflection. I turn on the faucet and splash some water in my face, hoping to start anew, and then I pat myself down with a thin, dry paper towel, just before I return to the conference room.

When I walk in, I see a man who wasn't there before, and my eyes fly open wide. He is wearing a dark tailored suit with a red tie. My heart becomes a racehorse, running faster and faster to win the Kentucky Derby. It can't be. How can it be? Surely my eyesight is failing me. Surely he is not who I think he is.

But he is. It's Chris. *My* Chris. As in the Chris who kissed me at Uhuru Peak. He is dressed in a suit and tie, very debonair.

"Hello, Marren."

What?

His eyes meet mine. I have no idea what to say or what to do. But then I say exactly what I'm thinking.

"What are you doing here?"

"...we should talk outside," he says. "If you'll excuse us—"

"...here, Chris?"

"...ever a good time. I'm

—"

to d...

I know why.

I'm not the right person for this. I can t.

I rise from my chair and bolt out the door, and Chr...

We are in a game of cat and mouse, a sudden spectacle of sorts.

"Marren, please stop! I can explain."

I run past the front desk, past the daisies and lilies and the receptionist who so graciously led us back to our meeting room. I can see the confused look on her face as I whiz by, making a beeline for the front door. Just as I exit the building, Chris catches up to me.

"Don't do this. I never wanted things to be like this. You have to know that."

I close my eyes and feel the tears begin to stream down my face. My pain manifests itself in the form of loud, deep sobs. I place my face in my hands.

"Marren, I'm sorry. I'm really, really sorry about all of this. I had no idea that I would meet someone like you on that mountain. That we would find ourselves in such precarious positions. I know the pain that you've been through. I can't tell you how terrible this has been for me to think I've made it worse."

I look up from my emotional breakdown. "Why didn't you tell me? Why hasn't anyone told me anything? My in-laws didn't tell me about the lawsuit, you didn't tell me the truth about what you really do for a living, and Brody didn't tell me about his addiction to those awful little pills. How am I supposed to trust anyone or anything, ever again?"

His eyes go cold. I can tell he doesn't have a good answer. But I do.

"Leave me alone, Chris. I'll go back in and finish the deposition, but I will never once trust you again. You're nothing but a fraud. A deceiver."

He looks down at the ground, his expression full of defeat. "I'm sorry you feel that way," he says, looking up again. "Listen, I really like you, Marren. And I'm sorry things ended the way they did in Africa. But I've got a job to do, and I have to do it to the best of my ability. I owe it to my clients."

He walks back into the building, as if I've never even met him.

I am left standing alone in that parking lot, my whole future just crumbling. Suddenly, I am trapped inside a building decimated by the most devastating of earthquakes. I am buried under the rubble, slowly dying, and yet I'm still alive. There is little to no hope that anyone will find me and save me.

I'm a chameleon, and I can't find the right color.

I sulk back to the conference room and take my seat again, trying to pretend I hadn't just done what I did. Kayla and Sam are awkwardly silent. Tara asks me if I'm okay to continue. She explains that we can delay if we need to. I shake my head. I'm here to put this behind me.

Chris slides on a pair of reading glasses, something I never saw him wear on the mountain. I wonder if his vision has deteriorated since. My vision of him certainly has.

"Mrs. Halleck," he begins, and his stoic tone catches me off guard. I'm supposed to be Marren from Arkansas, the one who fell asleep in his arms inside of a tent on Mount Kilimanjaro. But the way he's speaking suggests that we don't know each other at all.

"I'm sorry I was running late today," Chris says as he straightens his tie and looks over at Sam. "Thank you, Sam, for taking the reins until I could make it." He clears his throat. "Anyway, I have some ' ~uestions for you, if you're ready."

~~t believe I am sitting here, across from

~~t of all of this. Now,

"Did you ever ს.ɪ.

prescription, to maybe try to relax.

I can't believe what I'm hearing. How could ιιι. _ what to say.

"Just answer the question, Mrs. Halleck. Yes or no."

Tara intervenes. Her gold earrings glisten under the fluorescent conference room lighting. "Objection," she says. "That's irrelevant. This lawsuit is about Brody Halleck, not my client."

"Fine," Chris says smugly. "I'll rephrase the question. Mrs. Halleck, isn't it true that both you and your husband *misused* these pills? I mean, you don't light a match and throw it on the floor, do you? You're supposed to use it *correctly*. And if you do, it's safe, right?"

I look at Tara again. She nods, suggesting that it's okay for me to answer.

"I guess," I say.

"All right," Chris says, shuffling his paperwork and taking off his readers. "Mrs. Halleck, were you aware that your husband was meeting other hydrocodone users for something called 'downer parties'?"

I narrow my eyes. This is the first I've ever heard of this.

Chris slaps a piece of paper in front of me.

"This is a sworn affidavit from a woman named Heather Hammond," he says. "She says that she and Mr. Halleck regularly met together with at least two other people to take pills and 'hang out' together while they were high."

My eyes widen again.

"Mrs. Halleck, were you aware of this?" Chris demands.

His question slices through me, cutting a vital cord inside of me. I bleed emotion internally. I picture Brody, taking pills with people I've never seen or met, sharing in their own sad euphoria, engaging with them instead of me.

I look at Tara, just before I stand up.

"I'm sorry. I can't do this right now," I say, and I leave the room again, this time calmly. When I walk through the door, Chris's chokehold is gone, and I can breathe again. There is no way I can relive all of this. No way I can allow this man—the one who was so wonderful to me on the mountain—to unearth pain I didn't even know I could feel.

That's it. I'm done. And I never want to see Chris Courtland again.

64

I'VE ᴅᴇ

months now. Trish couᴅᴅ

and I've found my color.

For the first few weeks after my visit to New Orleaɴ,
coattails of my Kilimanjaro high, sailing through each day with a
smile on my face and a pen in my hand, writing my way through
the pain. I tried to impress the hell out of everyone around me—at
least those who were still speaking to me after the kiss picture. I had
to show them that, finally, after losing everything and going to that
mountain to find it, the new me was *okay*.

Except I wasn't. I still saw Brody in my dreams. I still longed for
my parents. *And then I discovered the real Chris—the one who serves as lead
counsel for the company that made the drug that killed my husband.* Three different types of unrelenting grief, a daunting road to travel.

If I learned anything from Kilimanjaro, it's that I cannot journey through life alone. The new me needed guidance. So I called
Greta, hoping to find some.

Greta is a blessing. She moved to Clear Springs from Little Rock,
where she earned her master's degree in social work, with a specialty

in grief counseling. She lost her mother to cancer at a young age, and she understands everything that I've been telling her. There's something special about trauma that binds broken hearts and helps them to heal faster. The support of someone who truly *understands* your heartache is the best kind of medicine.

I've told Greta *everything*—all about Brody, all about my parents, and of course, all about Chris. I am grieving Chris differently than Brody or my parents, because he is still here. At least I think he is. I can only hope he is, in spite of everything.

Greta is sympathetic to my obsession with Chris, but does her best to steer me away from my thoughts of him, guiding me in the direction of that which I can control. We say the serenity prayer together a lot. Still, there's not a day that goes by where I don't think of picking up the phone and calling him. Texting him. Emailing him. Greta has advised me against it, and so far, I've heeded her advice. "You need things in your life that will help you to heal, not hurt," she says. "Things that make your life easier, not harder."

My mind agrees. I wish my heart would too.

The best thing about Greta is that she champions my writing. Putting words on a page helps me to heal, not hurt. It makes my life easier, not harder. Creating a story, in the words of the serenity prayer, gives me the serenity to accept the things I cannot change, the courage to change the things I can, and the wisdom to know the difference.

I wish I started seeing Greta sooner.

▲ ▲ ▲

I'm currently attempting to write a novel. It's about a woman who loses her husband and then moves to Tanzania to start a whole new life. *Write what you know*, I've always read. In so many ways, this story is exactly what I know. But there's also much to learn. Like my life, the words come together beautifully one day, but on others, I struggle to find them. Greta tells me that on the days when the words won't come, I should go back and read my article in *Ladies Outdoor*.

"You can do it, Marren," she says. "You've been published before. You'll be published again."

I follow Greta's advice and reread my article:

Five Things I Learned

human op.
just as we need water or food ‿
to summit Kilimanjaro alone, I would surely have ‿‿
Were it not for the encouragement of my climbing team,
I would have turned back. Given up. The presence of my
fellow climbers and support staff was key to my success.

2. **Pole, pole.** This is a Swahili saying that is popular with
   many guides on Kilimanjaro. It means "slowly, slowly."
   An easy and slow approach is calming and reassuring, allowing for a more careful, less chaotic technique
   that is more likely to result in success. Keep this in mind
   for anything, friends: a measured perspective is much
   more likely to succeed than a rushed, haphazard one.
   Remember to take things ever so slowly, no matter what
   you do.

3. **There is beauty in the simplicity of life.** So many of us
   equate happiness with becoming rich and famous and
   living lavish, rock-star lifestyles. On a journey to the
   summit of Kilimanjaro, happiness is a simple day on the

mountain, telling stories, eyeing nature, chanting and singing and spending time with members of your climbing team. There, it is the simpler things in life that are most fulfilling and rewarding.

4. **Passion is fuel for the soul.** When you're passionate about something or someone, this drive calls you out of bed each day and provides you with motivation to care about your actions. On Kilimanjaro, my passion to get to the top of the mountain, coupled with a passion for one particular climber in my group, someone who encouraged me the entire way, was what actually propelled me to the summit.

5. **In life, you must keep going.** Winston Churchill once said, "If you're going through hell, keep going." Every day is critical. You must not stop. As Churchill also warned, "Never, ever, ever give up." You must continue the journey, or, as they say in Swahili: *Safari lazima iendelee.* The journey must continue.

When I'm finished reading, I smile to myself. *You did it, Marren.*

I've done it. I've conquered a mountain. I've conquered my fear of failure in writing. And the new me will keep conquering this crazy thing called life, again and again.

65

push the s

"Good morning," he says.

granted Frasier Industries' motion for summa. ,
Effectively, they have won. There will be no hearing on the merits.
We can appeal it, but Tara isn't enthusiastic about our chances of
winning. She's calling me in a few minutes, and I'd like to patch you
in. Is that okay?"

I close my eyes. I'm not sure I can take this again. I don't want
to think about Brody and our scarred past anymore. I don't want to
think of Chris and the possibility of facing him in court. Nevertheless,
I agree.

A few minutes later, I am on a conference call with Tara, George,
and Trish, discussing the path forward in our fight against Frasier
Industries.

"What I'm about to say might surprise you," Tara says. Her
voice is steady, seemingly unshaken by what's happened thus far.
"Ordinarily, I would urge you to appeal the court's decision to grant

summary judgment. But this case is special, and my job is to lead you to victory."

There is an awkward silence among us.

"Here's what I propose," she begins. "To truly defeat the drug companies, we need regulatory reform. Monetary relief from a single case is not necessarily going to change the face of opioid abuse in the future. What will change things are changes in the rules."

Another strange silence.

"If I were you, I would change the trajectory of my battle. I'd fight through the foundation to get the regulatory changes made that can truly make a difference."

"So we just give up?" George says. "I can't do that. I won't give up without a fight."

"You're certainly not giving up by deciding not to appeal, Mr. Halleck," Tara says. "You are just taking a different route to get to the same destination. Think of me as your Waze app. I'm just advising you to take a different route. The one that will actually get you there more quickly than the other ones."

66

a beautiful, baby-blu~ ~
my coffee, contemplating what will happen ~~ ~
my novel. My thoughts roam. Possible storylines burgeon, and my
fingers hit the keyboard wildly. I begin to type out the first words
that rage through my head, knowing that revision will soon be
necessary.

I am deep into chapter thirty when the doorbell rings.

I rise from my morning workspace, my hair tossed back in a
messy bun, glasses still clinging to the bridge of my nose, masking
under-eye circles made worse by my constant lack of sleep. I've yet
to shower and am flaunting my grungiest plaid pajama bottoms,
paired with a white undershirt. The coffee clearly hasn't roused me
enough to realize that a potentially embarrassing encounter could
ensue with whomever waits outside of my front door.

The doorbell rings again, and my bare feet trudge along the
unswept wooden floor, probably collecting mounds of dirt particles.

I hate having dirty feet, but I've been too busy writing to sweep. I'll have to do it later.

I turn the deadbolt to unlock the door, cracking it open slowly. I expect to see Trish, popping by for a midmorning visit. Or maybe the book that I've most recently ordered from Amazon, sitting there on my doorstep, waiting for me to retrieve it.

But when I open the door completely, I am stunned by what I see. A pair of hazel eyes under a weathered cowboy hat. Expensive-looking cowboy boots. That incredible smile.

My mouth drops open.

"Hello, Marren," he says.

I am silenced by shock. The morning-blue of his eyes, despite being subdued in the shadow of his cowboy hat, seduces me.

Chris.

At first, I am a mixed bag of emotions. Part of me is so happy to see him that I want to throw my arms around him, kiss him in the same way that he kissed me at the Kilimanjaro summit that day. The other part is enraged by the fact that he's not the man I thought he was. I think of the conference room again, the way he forced me back into my painful past. The way I never wanted to see him again.

Words fail me. I am momentarily captivated by each segment of his handsome appearance—a patch of gray scruff along the edges of his chin, his broad shoulders sitting atop a well-toned frame, hair that curls out gently from underneath his hat. I have no idea what to say.

"What are you doing here?" I ask.

"I figured you'd say that," he says, fiddling with his hat. "The truth is I don't know. But I'm here, and I'd like to talk to you if that's okay."

I can feel the redness rising to the top of my cheeks. "If you don't know why you're here, then there's nothing for us to talk about. So long, Chris."

I slam the door shut and lean back against it, feeling the tears as they flood my eyes. I bring a hand to my head as I begin to bawl. He's here, after all this time, and I've slammed the door in his face? What have I done?

The right thing, my mind assures me.

Suddenly, there's a loud knock at the door. And then a pounding.

"Please, Marren," Chris says, his voice muffled but audible. "Please let me in. I'm so sorry. God, you don't know how sorry I ～ ᴛ should have invited you to go with me on that safari. I should ⁓⁓ ⁓nd how I really felt instead of being ⁓ ⁓⁓ me. I . . . I,

appropriate conᴠᴇ...

he points to the couch. "May I sit down: ᴫᴄ ⁓

I nod. When he is settled into the tufted fabric of Trish's latest find, he takes a long, deep breath and exhales loudly.

"First of all, you should know that I withdrew from the Frasier Industries case. And I've officially left the firm. I've decided to focus on the family business now. For Pete. And for you."

My eyes widen. *For me?*

He then brandishes a magazine, something he has obviously been carrying in his hands the whole time but I had yet to notice until now.

He holds the magazine—an issue of *Ladies Outdoor*—upright in the air. "I read your article, Marren," he says. "There's something I want to say to you, and I'm just so damn sorry it's taken me this long."

My nerves tangle into a ball as I sit on the sofa next to him, terrified of what's coming next. I run an anxious hand across my unwashed, pulled-into-a-messy-bun hair, embarrassed by my appearance, yet so elated by Chris's surprise announcement that I almost don't care.

"Your number four spoke to me," he says. "The one about passion being fuel for the soul. I've had a lot of time to think since we last talked. All this time spent alone, without you, has made me realize that—"

"That what?" I interrupt.

"That I wasn't passionate about my work as a lawyer. I was passionate about you. *You* are what fuels my soul. And I don't want to be without you anymore. I've tried. And things are just better when you are around. I want to share everything with *you*. My camera. My life. I love you, Marren Halleck."

I cannot believe what I am hearing. He steps closer to me and takes my face into his hands, just before he gently removes my glasses. For a moment, I panic about my appearance. But then I think of his betrayal, and anger summons an indifference to what I look like.

I want to push him away, but I cannot. Even anger can't fend off my attraction to him. His lips meet mine, and my knees buckle. I can't believe this is happening, after all this time of thinking that it never would. I worry about my appearance again, but then I recall that he's seen me on a mountain, my face sweaty and make-up free, my hair blown into a rat's nest from winds powerful enough to delay our summit. *Me at my most natural.*

This is what true love must really feel like. Someone who loves you at your most natural, in spite of your flaws. Just like Brody once did.

Or did he?

When guilt creeps up into me, I hear Greta's voice, telling me that it's okay to move on. *The real Brody would want you to be loved like this*, she says.

shoulder little black dress and simply / take me somewhere exciting that I've never been before, just as he has promised.

"Dress up," Chris told me. And so I did.

When I open the door, I am surprised to see George and Trish, standing together with Chris on my front porch. For a moment, I am bothered. Worried, even.

Why are George and Trish here? Is something wrong? The looks on their faces are somewhat somber, and I cannot read them as well as I would like to.

Oh, no.

Paranoia takes hold of me. Something bad has obviously transpired, or the three of them wouldn't be standing here in front of me on the porch, looking so pensive.

"Do you mind if we come in?" Chris says with a straight face. His tone is full of apathy.

I motion them inside.

Minutes later, we are seated in the family room, staring at each other uncomfortably. I want to offer them something to drink, an appetizer, to do something hospitable, and yet I'm too anxious to do so.

George speaks first.

"Marren, we all know how difficult your journey has been."

He pauses briefly and looks at Trish, who cannot take her eyes off me.

"We also know how much progress you have made . . . including your trip to Kilimanjaro. We've watched you struggle to keep going after losing your parents and Brody, to persevere in the most formidable of circumstances. And lately, we've watched you find happiness again. With this wonderful man sitting next to me."

Hope springs up inside of me. What is George about to say?

"Today, Chris came to ask us a question. He wanted to know if we'd give him permission to ask you something very important. He wanted to make sure it was okay by us. Okay by Brody."

I get chills as I wait for George to continue.

"Chris, take it from here," George says.

I look over at Trish, who hasn't moved a muscle. She is staring hard at me, concentrating. Sitting in her conservative boat-neck top and black pants, laser-focused on what will happen next, like she is watching a blockbuster movie, dying to know how it ends.

Chris walks over to me, dressed in khaki pants and a tailored white button-down, the hazel green in his eyes causing me to become lost in them.

He drops to one knee, and I swear I'm going to faint.

He reaches into his pocket and produces a box containing the most beautiful princess-cut diamond ring I've ever seen, alongside a black, porous volcanic rock. Just before he speaks, he looks over at George for a silent permission, and George nods.

"Marren Halleck," he says, offering the volcanic rock first. "This rock isn't pretty. But it's special." He hands it to me, and I hold it in my hand, feeling its rough outer edges. Clearly, it's a piece of rock from our journey to summit Kilimanjaro—one that resembles the rocks from the scree that had me tumbling to the ground. "It's the reason that you and I are together today. It's what commemorates our trip to the top of that mountain, our journey to summit Kilimanjaro together. We had to go through a lot of ugliness in our individual lives to get to the beautiful place we're at now."

His speech is so eloquent that it elicits some sort of happy com-

who has a single tear

"Yes!" I say.

Chris takes me into his arms and presses his lips to mine in the most passionate kiss that I think we've ever shared. George and Trish embrace, wiping tears from their usually composed faces. Suddenly, they break into an unexpected applause.

Chris whispers that he loves me into my ear, and George touches my arm. I turn to him, listening as he begins to speak.

"Chris came to ask me for my blessing today, Marren. He came to make sure that it was appropriate for him to ask for your hand in marriage. Trish and I are beyond thrilled. Brody would want nothing less for you."

George produces a bottle of champagne from out of the blue, like how a magician pulls a rabbit from a hat. The cork pops off, and bubbles flow everywhere as Trish gathers glasses for each of us.

"Congratulations, Marren and Chris!"

68

THE WEDDING WILL BE IN SAINT LUCIA, an island nation in the eastern Caribbean. But instead of a typical resort venue, Chris and I make a pact: we'll unite in holy matrimony on the summit of Gros Piton, a small mountain on Saint Lucia's western coast that stands at 2,620 feet—hardly a percentage of the challenge we tackled when we first met on our journey to 19,341 feet—the top of Kilimanjaro. It is a common goal that we both share—*getting married on a mountain.*

▲ ▲ ▲

On a particularly cool morning in late June, Chris's private jet races down the runway at Dallas Love Field, ever so gently rising into partly cloudy skies. As we gain altitude, I notice Chris's strikingly handsome grin. I'm sure that he is thinking about the plane and how proud he is to own it. He just bought it last month, and he loves it like a doting father who adores his newborn baby.

The flight to Hewanorra International Airport in Saint Lucia is rather turbulent—my anxiety runs high, and I am hopeful that this is not a sign of things to come. I sip champagne, at times grasping my glass for dear life as Chris holds my other hand. Something about his fingers being intertwined with mine is reassuring, even more so than the alcohol. Finally, the turbulence subsides, and I relax. I put my headphones in and listen to "Someday" by Rob Thomas, thinking how the lyrics that Brody loved for so long are actually coming to life, without him. Guilt finds me again.

I think of the judgment I'll get, moving on this fast. It's been only a year and a half since Brody died. I picture Colette McSwain and ˙ ˡˡ˔ⁿᵈ hᵢₘ. the fighting words she once said to me.

¹ ⁻⁻⁻ dead a year, and you're chas-

nonfiction paperback, ᵗʰᵉ ʷᵃʸ
think of Greta's advice.

The real Brody would want me to be loved.

We touch down in Saint Lucia, and I decide that Greta is right. I'm going to marry Chris Courtland, and I'm going to be loved.

69

I WAKE TO THE SOUND of crashing waves and singing birds. Chris wraps his muscular arms around me, planting a kiss on the back of my head. We snuggle for a while as he gently rubs my back. For a moment, I forget that this is our big day.

We fall asleep again together for a brief time, maybe an hour or so, and when we rise, the sun is shining so brightly that it forces us out of bed. I go out on the porch to study the sunlit ocean in the distance, and Chris starts the coffee. Thirty minutes later—just one cup of coffee in—I'm dressed in a simple white Lululemon workout top and black leggings, nothing like the attire of a traditional bride.

Soon after, the taxi driver picks us up from Cap Maison, a resort in the northernmost part of Saint Lucia known as Cap Estate, where we are staying. It is early, 6:45 a.m., and I've barely gained enough lucidity from my morning coffee to function. Chris, on the other hand, is a morning person. Dressed in sleek, cool climbing attire and armed with a large water bottle, he is raring to go. Our driver, Melvin, talks nonstop, telling stories and gesturing wildly as he speeds around sharp corners along steep embankments. I find myself closing my eyes, praying, hoping that we will make it to the mountain safely.

My left hand, now clammy with anxiety, is decorated with my elegant engagement ring and firmly lodged in Chris's hand. There is an uncomfortable tickle in my stomach as Melvin takes another curve. One false move and we are off the edge of a cliff. I envision us plummeting to our deaths down the edge of a rocky ridge, just before our wedding ceremony. Chris must sense the tension inside of me, because he tells another one of his corny jokes.

"Hey, Marren, why are mountains always so tired?"

~~~ ~~nchline.

on some history. ~~~ ~~

nated at *Fond Gens Libre*, or the "Valley of the Free People ~~~ ~~ founded by descendants of enslaved people who'd sought shelter at the peak after fleeing from plantation owners. When Melvin finishes his story, Chris gives him a generous tip, then Melvin drives away smiling. I like Melvin, but I detest his driving. I'm happy that we made it here.

We meet our personal guide, Lucian, at an arid clubhouse-type structure where we are able to use the restrooms and gather our gear. Lucian is a medium-sized, very thin man, with light-brown skin and a very long, dark beard. He is wearing a simple green T-shirt, khaki shorts, and a red baseball cap. His accent is thick and Jamaican-like.

We follow Lucian along the trail, which at first is a very easy, level climb. The terrain is mostly forest, a bit like the rainforest on Kilimanjaro, except not quite as striking. Along this particularly simple portion of the journey, Chris takes my hand again, as he often does, and we admire the scenery—flowers like orchids and anthuriums, birds like parrots and black finches and orioles, and some very unique lizards. As we make our way higher, I become strangely calmer, for it feels like an easier version of our previous journey, something like "Kilimanjaro light."

We continue to climb, and the terrain gets a little steeper and rockier. Like Simon, Lucian narrates along the way. He tells us that, while English is the official language, a vast majority of Saint Lucia residents also speak Creole, a local language also known as Patwa or Patois. He says that it is similar to French, and it dates back to the French colonization of the island, all the way to the sixteenth and seventeenth centuries. According to Lucian, the main sources of local economic prosperity are bananas, coconuts, cacao, citrus fruits, and fishing. I am fascinated by Lucian's accent, as well as the ease with which Chris and I are making our way forward, hand in hand.

At the halfway point, we stop for a quick break. A middle-aged woman is there with a man that—from the huge diamond on her left hand—I assume is her husband. She is very sweaty, breathing hard, and telling the man next to her that she doesn't think she can continue. She needs to turn around, she says. I, too, am sweaty and winded, but there's no turning back now. I am much too determined to become Chris Courtland's wife. I watch him now, taking more pictures, just as he did in Africa. I think of how patient and kind he was when he showed me how to take pictures with his camera on Mount Kilimanjaro. I think of the way we fell asleep together in the tent on the mountain, his arms protecting me from that awful wind. And I can't help but think of the way he gave up his big-shot legal career to pursue me and support my personal convictions.

When he's done taking pictures, he turns around and smiles. Then he walks over to me, camera in hand, and speaks words that motivate me even more.

"I love you, Marren from Arkansas," he tells me. "I can't wait to marry you at the top of this mountain."

▲ ▲ ▲

An hour later, we are mere feet from the summit. I carefully select each step as I reminisce on the journey we've encountered thus far: steep, wall-like places where I feared falling backward; rocky, sharp terrain where I imagined slipping and cutting myself open, the blood gushing too fast for a wedding to ensue; and finally, the ˡ ·ᵛʰᵉʳᵉ I panic about the things we'll

out a script and ᵛᵍₒ

sure that our guide was also an officiant of the government ᵤₗ ᵤₗₗₗₗ Lucia. We take vows, right here on the top of Gros Piton, sweating to the sound of promises to forsake all others and to remain faithfully united in sickness and in health. Finally, as the sun blazes in the noon sky, Lucian pronounces us man and wife, and Chris places a hand on my cheek. His lips land gently on mine as he kisses me deeply, passionately, like we're on top of the world. And in a way, we are. It is a love that began on Kilimanjaro and has been cemented here on Gros Piton.

We are now Mr. and Mrs. Chris Courtland, forever bound by the mountains that we have climbed.

70

CHRIS RAISES A GLASS of sparkling cider in honor of our one-year wedding anniversary. We've both given up alcohol in honor of Brody. Our celebration is extra special tonight, because it's also the night of the inaugural Brody Halleck Foundation's Rising Above Gala. For the last nine months, Trish and I have worked tirelessly on the foundation's Rising Above project, which helps recovering addicts and sponsors drug-free trips to Mount Kilimanjaro. Our very first crew will depart for Africa in just a few weeks. Chris is going to go with them. I wish I could too, but I am expecting our very first baby Courtland.

After dinner, it is time for me to rise and speak to the crowd of attendees. My simple black evening gown looks like it is stretched over a basketball. I waddle up to the stage as gracefully as I can and adjust the microphone attached to the podium. All eyes are on me. My hand shakes a little as the baby kicks. I work to stay focused, to remember what it is that I'm planning to say.

"Good evening, ladies and gentlemen," I begin. I look at Chris, who is extremely handsome in his tuxedo tonight. His smile reassures me, pushes my speech along.

"I'm Marren Halleck Courtland, one of the founders of the Brody Halleck Foundation. We're so glad you could be here tonight for our inaugural event. As you know, we created the foundation in honor of my late husband, Brody Halleck, who lost his battle with addiction almost two years ago. Brody would have loved the fact that all of you are here to support us tonight. So thank you, again."

I go on to explain the Rising Above project and talk about my Kilimanjaro adventure. I say that the foundation has raised over $500,000 in its first year and that we are doing great things to fund the fight against addiction. Again and again, the applause rolls

parents, and ...

Although these chairs are empty, my life and table are full.

71

I ANSWER THE DOOR in a pair of black cowboy boots that Chris bought for me, my attempt to give our out-of-town guests a proper Texas welcome. The heat of the Texas summer hits me like a thick fog, and I can only imagine what my hair is doing now. Frizzing, fraying under the soupy humidity of the day.

As annoyed as I am by the sweltering weather, I am more elated to see the two women that are standing in front of me—one of them holding a precious, curly-headed baby girl dressed in a smocked bubble outfit and a tiny bow. Her bib is monogrammed with her initials, a gift from Chris and me. I lean in for a hug, and Leslie throws one arm around me. When our embrace ends, she extends her other arm, which is holding a large, rectangular-shaped, wrapped present.

"Open it," Leslie insists.

I tear into the beautiful gold wrapping paper, awed by what I find. It is a painting of Kilimanjaro, full of purple and brown and orange hues rising above a golden Serengeti landscape.

"We had it commissioned," Leslie explains as she looks at Seri. "And we hope that it will always remind you of our time together on the mountain. We had the same one done after we summited last year."

I fight tears. Seri blows me a kiss as she holds the baby girl. Instinctively, I reach for this tiny little being, unable to take my eyes off her curls. Seri smiles as she hands her over to me. I bounce her on my hip. She is simply perfect.

Chris grills lunch for us in our outdoor kitchen while we set up a play area for the babies—the curly-haired, doe-eyed girl and the feisty, blue-eyed boy, who is just two months younger. They crawl around, each of them old enough to sit on their own now, exchang- ... Leslie's staunch fear of germs), exploring

We shar- ...

advice.

I look down at our sweet babies, who are so preciously playing together. Simone, nine months, daughter of Seri and Leslie, and Peter (aka PJ), my son with Chris, seven months. The only thing that could make this occasion more perfect is if they were wearing onesies that read, "Kili Me Softly," like Claire and Casey's T-shirts. I miss Claire and Casey, who couldn't be here because their twins are due next week.

Our Kilimanjaro crew is a family of sorts, born of a mountain.

Safari lazima iendelee.

The journey must continue.

ACKNOWLEDGMENTS

along on this harrowing journey to publication with me, for reading every crappy draft and giving me honest feedback, for listening to me complain about how hard this has been, for giving me a shoulder to cry on and an encouraging "don't give up" on the days when I thought I wasn't good enough to be a writer. Your love has been the catalyst for my success; you're like fresh water to flowers, helping them to grow. You are truly one of the good guys, a rare find. I love you more than words can say.

To my children—all six of you, bonus and biological. Goodness, you've listened to me talk about writing a book for years now. I'm sure you've rolled your eyes when I wasn't looking, thinking, *Won't she just shut-up about this and get the darn thing published?* Okay, I'm kidding! But seriously, thank you all for your support and encouragement and for listening to me and reading my work when I know you had better things to do on Snapchat and Instagram. LOL! Love you all so much and couldn't be prouder of each of you.

To my mother-in-law and father-in-law, for raising a good man who had the courage to do something so incredible that it inspired a story like this. Thank you for being the good people that you are. Thank you for supporting me on this journey called life and for showing me what true, unconditional love really looks like. I love you both with my whole heart.

To my amazing critique partner, Elizabeth Lewis, who is just one of the best people I know. I can't thank you enough for all of your insight and legal advice for the story. Cheers to former lawyers who are now writers!

To my beta readers for this book and previous manuscripts that have yet to be published, I owe you big. Your feedback has most certainly made me a better writer!

To my writer friend Karen Vine Fuller, for all you have done to encourage and connect me to other writers along the way. You are a ray of sunshine. I love you, and the world needs more people like you.

To some of my very best friends who've been there for me for all of life—through the wonderful and the awful, from the teenage years and beyond—you all have never failed to support and encourage me in my writing journey. Katie, Calhoon, Jill, and Allison, I love you all so much. I cannot thank you enough for being there when I needed you most and for your constant love and encouragement.

To my friend Andrea, who saw me through the best of times and the worst of time as an expat in Singapore so many years ago now. You and your family are so very special to me. Thank you for all you have done to love and support me over the years! You are the truest kind of friend, and I am ever so thankful for you and your gift of taking care of others. Much love.

To my editors for this book, Ava, Lee, and Lindsey—you made a good story great. I cannot thank you enough!

To my publishing team at Greenleaf Book Group, wow. Words are not enough. Thank you for making my dreams come true! Y'all are just plain awesome!

To everyone who is reading this section right now, because without readers, a story is lifeless, with no meaning or impact.

To those who are currently struggling with or have struggled with addiction, as well as those who have loved ones who have battled addiction, please know that you are not alone, and I hope this book will encourage you to find a support structure that can help you break free from the prison of secrets and shame. Prayers for

ABOUT
THE AUTHOR

Graduate College of Social Work. Originally from Arkansas, she currently resides in Texas with her husband and children. *Somewhere Above It All* is her first novel.